A Boy
Called
HOPELESS

A BOY
Called
HOPELESS

by
M. J.

A DAVID MELTON NOVEL

LANDMARK EDITIONS, INC.
Kansas City, Missouri

29084.

Seventh Printing

COPYRIGHT © 1976 and 1986   David Melton

Library of Congress Cataloging in Publication Data

Melton, David.
    A boy called hopeless.

    SUMMARY: Fifteen-year-old Mary Jane describes her family's reactions when they discover that her younger brother is brain injured and their decision to participate in a program of rehabilitation together.
    [1. Mentally handicapped—Fiction.   2. Brain-damaged children—Fiction]   I. Title.
PZ7.M5164Bo   1986   [Fic]   86-27557

    ISBN 0-933849-32-X (LIB.BDG.)
    ISBN 0-933849-07-9 (pbk.)

Jacket and book design by David Melton

Landmark Editions, Inc.
1420 Kansas Avenue
Kansas City, Missouri 64127

Printed in the United States of America

Dedication

To Glenn J. Doman, Gretchen Kerr, Elaine
Lee, Art Sandler, Sandra Brown, Meg Tyson,
Dr. Edward LeWinn, Dr. Roselise Wilkinson,
Dr. Evan Thomas, Dr. Robert Doman, Hazel
Doman, Pearl LeWinn, Greta Erdtmann,
and the staff members of
The Institutes for the
Achievement of Human Potential
who work so valiantly to help make
brain-injured children well.

And to the brothers and sisters of brain-injured
children who so freely give their time, their
encouragement, and their love to these hurt ones.
What heroes they truly are.

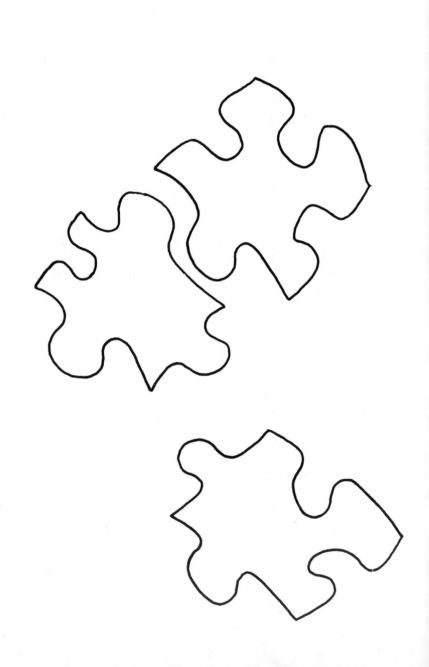

Contents

Contents (continued)

Acknowledgments

I am grateful to Gretchen Kerr and Elaine Lee for supplying stacks of case histories and helping me in the research for this book.

For allowing me to spend hours in their offices observing their work with brain-injured children and their parents, I am indebted to Glenn J. Doman, Art Sandler, Sandra Brown, Meg Tyson, Dr. Evan Thomas, Dr. Roselise Wilkinson, Dr. Robert Doman, and Hazel Doman.

For sharing the stories of their children's lives with me and for answering any and all questions I asked, I thank the many parents of brain-injured children whom I have met. I have nothing but enormous respect for their strength and their courage.

I also thank the brothers and sisters of these children who often travel thousands of miles with their families to seek help. I have been told that when parents spend so much time with one child other children in the family become resentful and have psychological problems. People who say such things should visit The Institutes and meet these brothers and sisters and find out how wrong such statements are. I have found these children to be happy, well adjusted youngsters who are concerned about their hurt brother or sister. Often, they appear much more mature than other children their age.

And I certainly appreciate the parents who allowed me to use their child's medical history in developing the story of Jeremiah Rodgers.

I thank my wife, Nancy, for typing the manuscript and for her many insights as a mother, a wife, and an editor. I am grateful to our daughter, Teresa, whose nimble penmanship constructed M.J.'s notes, and to our son, Todd, whose creative felt tip brought M.J.'s drawings into being.

And last, but not least, I would like to thank M.J., whoever she is and wherever she might be.

9

David Melton —author and illustrator

David Melton is one of the most versatile and prolific talents on the literary and art scenes today. His literary works span the gamut of factual prose, analytical essays, newsreporting, magazine articles, features, short stories, poetry and novels in both the adult and juvenile fields. When reviewing his credits, it is difficult to believe that such an outpouring of creative efforts came from just one person. In seventeen years, twenty-four of his books have been published, several of which have been translated into a number of languages.

Mr. Melton has illustrated ten of his own books and three by other authors, while many of his drawings and paintings have been reproduced as fine art prints, posters, puzzles, calendars, book jackets, record covers, mobiles and note cards, and they have been featured in national publications.

Mr. Melton has also gained wide reputation as a guest speaker and teacher. He has spoken to hundreds of professional, social and civic groups, relating the problems that confront parents and teachers of learning-disabled and handicapped children, and he has influenced the mandates of change in the field of special education and therapies for brain-injured children. He is also a frequent guest on local and national radio and television talk shows.

Since a number of Mr. Melton's books are enjoyed by children, he has visited hundreds of schools nationwide as a principal speaker in Author-in-Residence Programs, Young Authors' Days, and Children's Literature Festivals. He also conducts in-service seminars for teachers and teaches professional writing courses throughout the country.

To encourage and celebrate the creativity of students, Mr. Melton has developed the highly acclaimed teacher's manual, WRITTEN & ILLUSTRATED BY..., which is used in thousands of schools in teaching students to write and illustrate original books by *THE MELTON METHOD*. To provide opportunities for students to become professionally published authors and illustrators, in association with Landmark Editions, Inc., he helped initiate THE NATIONAL WRITTEN & ILLUSTRATED BY... AWARDS CONTEST FOR STUDENTS.

Introduction

Although this book is a novel, and some of the characters are fictional, it is really a true story.

There is really a man named Glenn Doman.

Gretchen Kerr, Art Sandler, Meg Tyson, Elaine Lee, Sandra Brown, Dr. Evan Thomas, Dr. Robert Doman, and Dr. Edward LeWinn are real people.

And there really is a place in Philadelphia, Pennsylvania, called The Institutes for the Achievement of Human Potential.

Although the names of the other characters are fictional, their situation is true. The family in this story is a composite of many families. The characters of Mr. and Mrs. Rodgers are drawn from hundreds of parents of brain-injured children whom my wife and I have been fortunate to meet. We know them well, for like them, we too were parents of a brain-injured child.

M.J. and Josh are so much like the brothers and sisters of brain-injured children we have seen that every time we visit The Institutes we find ourselves wondering if we will see them there. Even at home, I sometimes reach for the phone to call them and ask how they are. Then I realize I don't know their number or where they live.

And as for Jeremiah. . . I have seen him, or children like him, more times than I care to count. What lovely and loving children they are. How very much in need of help they are. How unfair that they are ever called *hopeless*.

I am sure many will ask, "Did David Melton write this book or did M.J.?" I'm not sure. I know I typed it, but I don't know that I wrote it. Every time I started thinking it was mine, I heard a girl's voice saying in disgusted tones, "Now wait a minute! Whose book is this anyway . . .yours or mine?"

I wish I knew.

—David Melton

11

note—

This is a story about my family, but mostly it is about my youngest brother, Jeremiah.

Although there have been many incidents in Jeremiah's life which have been sad, and some have been tragic, I refuse to write about them with tears in my eyes because I am not that kind of person. Besides, I don't believe Jeremiah would like his story told in a dreary, sentimental way.

My name is Mary Jane Rodgers, but I prefer to be called M. J. (Mary Jane sounds like a girl with long golden curls and pinafores. I'm not that kind of person either.)

I'm fifteen now but the story began eight years ago.

M. J.

The Announcement

When Josh and I were told that we were to have a new brother or sister, I said, "Who needs it?"

As I saw it, either way it was bound to be more of a problem for me than it would be for Josh. If *it* was a girl, in a few short months part of my room would be cluttered with plastic toys and stacks of diapers. If *it* was a boy, I would still be expected to be a part-time nursemaid because older sisters usually get stuck in the helping-hand brigade.

I could imagine how it would be:

"M. J., will you see what the baby wants?"

"M. J., will you bring me the talcum powder?"

"M. J., will you take the baby for a walk?"

"M. J., will you. . ."

That would probably be my new name—*M. J. Willyou.*

The announcement came as a complete surprise. Since at the time I was seven and Josh was six, it never occurred to us that we might be threatened with the arrival of other rivals. We had simply taken it for granted that our family was finished.

It wasn't that Josh or I had anything against babies or anything like that. The timing was bad, that's all. Josh and I had reached certain understandings and agreements. After years of many arguments and numerous debates (sometimes ended by a quick right in the breadbasket or a left hook to the jaw), Josh and I had not exactly signed a final armistice, but we had settled on terms for a peaceful coexistence, such as knocking before entering one another's room. It was understood that we would go into the other's room *only* in case of fire, earthquake, or some other unforeseen emergency. We would also not nudge one another with elbows or sharp objects when meeting in the hallway.

It was working out fairly well. On occasion we even spoke to each other.

We did not welcome the idea of having to define territories to a new member of the family. Neither did we feel we should be expected to give up any of our things to the new one. In short, we did not appreciate the prospect of receiving this "gift from heaven."

At least that was the way I felt. I'm sure Josh felt much the same way, but of course he didn't verbalize his thoughts so clearly. When Mother told us, Josh responded to the news with his usual shrug, but underneath his aimless gesture I could tell he was in a state of shock. He probably felt his own identity was being threatened.

After we were outside and away from Mother's ears, I told Josh that he could feel free to confide in me and tell me his innermost thoughts.

I never will forget how he turned to me, gave me his sullen look, and said, "My innermost thought is that you are probably the nosiest girl in the world."

Of course, now that I am eight years older and more mature, I realize I was attempting to toughen the skin of my ego to prepare for the competition that another child might bring. Although on the surface I was a bit resentful, there were moments when I found myself thinking what a joy it might be to have a "real live" baby in the house. Harder hearts than mine have been warmed by the face of a child.

Like it or not, the die was cast. We adopted the attitude of "what will be, will be."

If it had not been for the addition to our family, I probably never would have started this book. Until that time, our family was so everyday there would have been nothing to write worth reading. I

*could imagine a reader saying, "How dull,"
and closing the book with a listless thud.*

Mother is not a scientist, an alcoholic, a revolutionary, or any of those things that make a character breathlessly exciting. Although I think Mother is pretty, she is not the glamorous movie-star type. She is pretty in a quiet, friendly way and has a smile which is so warm and generous that she makes people around her feel happy to be with her. Don't get me wrong. She isn't Mary Poppins carrying a spoonful of sugar all the time. Indeed, she is not! Sometimes she loses her temper and yells at us. She can be very stern. Both Josh and I can testify from experience that Mother believes spanking is an acceptable form of discipline.

She reads a lot. She is a thoughtful and considerate person, and she loves fresh flowers. What makes Mother so extraordinary is that although she is quite unique, she appears to be ordinary. That fools many people who do not know her well.

Dad is the same, only different. Although they are the same age, Dad appears older. He is also quieter, except at parties. Then watch out—he knows a thousand jokes.

I don't think I know my father as well as I know my mother. Dad doesn't talk much about himself.

For the most part, I guess my father is like many other fathers. He works at the office. He likes to play golf, and he watches football on television.

Sometimes he can be a lot of fun. Sometimes he is very sweet and understanding. Sometimes he can be so cross and irritable that it's better to stay out of his way. If something has gone wrong at the office, we don't expect Mr. Nice Guy to come home.

There is one thing I would like to say about both my father and my mother. If I could pick any parents from the neighborhood, I would keep the ones I have.

Then, of course, there is Josh. . . .

I just hate books in which the author writes, "My brother is the dearest and sweetest human being in the whole wide world." Such drivel makes me want to throw up. If I ever wrote such a thing about Josh, he'd probably poke me in the eye.

No one in his right mind would write a book about Josh. Josh might make an interesting sentence or even a humorous paragraph, but he would not sustain reader interest for an entire chapter. A whole book about Josh would be completely out of the question because no one would read it—not even Josh.

If we lined up Josh with nine other boys and didn't make them take a bath, you couldn't tell one from the other. Until Josh was eight, I thought he had been born with grimy elbows and a band-aid on his left knee.

The closest thing in common which Josh and I ever had were our ages. We were only eleven months apart, which goes to prove that girls mature at a much faster rate than boys.

When I think back, I can remember having profound thoughts when I was Josh's age, and I asked important questions such as, "Who am I? Where am I going?" Not Josh. He *knows* who he is. He is a shortstop in the 3-2 League, and if he has his way, he is going to play baseball three times a week for the rest of his life.

Now I come to Jeremiah. . . .

I have to think how I can tell everything about him so that everyone will really understand why he was the way he was and how all of our lives were changed because of him.

I'm not sure I can do that -- but I will try.

Named—Then Born

Mother was about five months pregnant when she first placed my hand on her rounded abdomen and said, "Keep your hand there and you'll feel the baby move."

I sat very quietly and waited. Suddenly I felt something ripple against my hand and both my mother and I laughed.

"What was that?" I asked.

"I don't know," Mother answered. "It was probably a knee or an elbow."

After that I felt more excited about the baby and Mother let me feel it move quite often. In fact, it was during one of these times that, sight unseen, I named Jeremiah.

I told Mother that I hoped *it* would be a girl and that if *it* was a girl, I wished she would name her Cassandra because I thought Cassandra sounded so poetic and lovely.

Mother smiled and asked, "And what if it's a boy?"

"It doesn't make any difference what you call a boy," I told her. "Joe, Jim, Jack, Jake, or anything." Then I stopped for a moment and I thought of the frontiersman we had talked about in school. Jeremiah Johnson—that seemed to be a good name for a boy, so I said, "If it's a boy, let's call him Jeremiah."

To my surprise, Mother said, "I like that—Jeremiah."

So from that time on every time Mother called me to feel a nudging elbow or moving knee, she said, "Jeremiah's at it again."

I knew my chances for a sister were fading fast because it was "Jeremiah this" and "Jeremiah that."

Mother told me that Jeremiah would be born in May, so I was more than surprised to find Mrs. Wilson, our next-door neighbor, waiting for Josh and me when we came home from school one Monday afternoon.

Mrs. Wilson told us, "Your mother is at the hospital and you will soon have a new brother or sister to play with."

"But it isn't May yet," I said. "It's only March fifteenth. It's too soon. Mother said it takes nine months for a baby to be ready. He won't be ready yet."

Although Mrs. Wilson told me not to worry, I did. I wondered what would happen if a baby was born before he was ready. I thought of all kinds of things. Maybe he wouldn't have an ear. Maybe his little toes wouldn't be there yet. Or perhaps his nose wouldn't be done. Oh no! I knew—I just knew that Josh and I were doomed to have the only brother in Indianapolis who didn't have a completed nose.

Those thoughts may sound silly, but to a seven-year-old girl an unfinished nose can be pretty important, especially if it is on the face of her very own brother.

After Dad came home that night and told us that we had a six-pound, two-ounce brother and that he was perfect in every way, I finally relaxed.

Little did we know then that there was still cause for concern. Jeremiah was not perfect in every way.

In truth, there was something wrong with Jeremiah. That *something* would change our lives, because that *something* was SOMETHING terrible!

Almost Too Good

The first nine months of Jeremiah's life were probably the most peaceful. But such bliss was not to be long lasting.

"I was looking in M. J.'s baby book today," Mother said to my father one evening. "She was sitting alone when she was *six* months old. Jeremiah doesn't sit up yet."

Dad looked up and thought about what she had said, and then looked back down at the newspaper.

"Robert," Mother said to him, "I looked at Josh's baby book, too. He was sitting alone at *seven* months."

"Some babies do things later than others," he shrugged.

"Why?" my mother asked.

"Why what?"

"Why do some babies do things such as sitting up later than other babies?"

"Because they do," he answered.

Suddenly Mother stood up and her voice became impatient. "I don't believe that," she said. "I don't believe that things happen just because they happen. I think there are reasons. I think M.J. sat up at six months because she was a bright, healthy baby. The same with Josh. But Jeremiah is nine months old and he's not able to sit alone and he doesn't hold his head up well. In fact he doesn't do any of the things that M. J. and Josh were doing at his age. And I'll tell you something else. It doesn't look as if he's going to be sitting up any time in the near future."

Mother's voice became very loud. "There is something wrong with Jeremiah, and I don't know what it is!"

For a moment, both of my parents looked extremely angry. My father stood up and walked outside, slamming the front door behind him. Mother ran into the bedroom; another door slammed shut. Josh and I could hear that she was crying.

We had heard our parents argue before— sometimes longer, sometimes louder—but this one had been a strange argument because it was practically no argument at all. They were both angry so quickly that neither Josh nor I could figure out what had happened or why Mother was so upset.

I tried to think back to the day that Mom and Dad brought Jeremiah home. We all agreed that he was a beautiful baby, and as Dad had said, he appeared to be perfect in every way.

Of course he was very small. His fingers were so tiny it was unbelievable that they could move. I wondered how they knew to grow fingernails.

Many times people say that when they see huge mountains or when they think of the vastness of space, they are overwhelmed by God's greatness. It's just the opposite with me. The big things don't surprise me at all because I expect God to work large miracles and create planets and stars and things like that. It's the little things that impress me with God. When I see a tiny spider weaving a web, I think *Wow, God must be wonderful to be able to make such a little thing with so many miniature parts!* Jeremiah's fingernails affected me the same way. I mean, it didn't surprise me that God could create babies, but what really impressed me was that he paid so much attention to detail.

During the first week, everything Jeremiah did fascinated both Josh and me. We watched him nurse, and bath times were a thousand delights.

I must admit that he was not nearly the trouble I thought he would be. I had expected that his constant crying would be a nuisance, but he cried very little.

He slept most of the time and it was quite peaceful in our house. Mother said he probably needed a lot of sleep because he had been born two months earlier than he was supposed to have been. That made sense. So I figured, *Wait till the end of the second month; suddenly he'll wake up and we'll see what havoc our brother can create.*

Two months went by. The third month passed. Jeremiah still slept most of the time, and when he was awake, he rarely cried.

"What a good baby he is," Mother would say. Then I noticed that she began adding to her statement, "almost too good."

One day I asked Mother, "What do you mean when you say, 'almost too good'?"

"Have I been saying that?" she asked. "I suppose I have," she answered herself.

"Well," she said, sitting down, "we expect babies to be some trouble because when they are very young they are completely helpless. We expect them to cry some and to make a fuss. If they cry too often, a mother tries to find out what makes her baby so uncomfortable. Crying is not only a signal to her from her baby, but some crying is good for the baby—it makes him breathe deeply and it helps his lungs to develop. But Jeremiah hardly ever cries, and by now I think he should be awake for longer periods of time."

"Maybe he's quiet because we keep him so comfortable," I suggested.

"I don't know," she said quietly. "We will ask the doctor next week."

Wait and See

Dr. Zefrelli was a tall, dark man who liked to tease kids.

"Mary Jane Rodgers," he said, looking over his glasses at me, "have you been pinching this baby?"

I could have died. I just knew that everyone in the waiting room heard his big mouth. My face got red as a beet. I ducked my head and followed Mother and Jeremiah into the doctor's office.

Sitting in a chair in the corner out of the way, I watched as Dr. Zefrelli examined my brother.

"Well, well, what a fine specimen. Okay. Nothing here—everything's all right there—hummm-uh, hun," Dr. Zefrelli mumbled. "Now then," he said turning to my mother, "what's the problem, Mrs. Rodgers?"

"He can't sit alone," my mother said in a rather nervous way.

"Well, I wouldn't worry about that," he replied. "You'll see. One of these days he'll sit up, cross his arms, and talk your leg off."

"He doesn't cry much either," Mother said.

"Well, you shouldn't complain about that," Dr. Zefrelli exclaimed. "I bet there are at least a half dozen mothers in that waiting room this very moment who will trade their squawling ones for your quiet one."

Mother smiled but she wasn't really amused.

"I don't think..." she started, hesitated, and then began again. "I don't think that Jeremiah is as alert as he should be."

"Mrs. Rodgers," the doctor said, "I wish I had a nickel for every new mother who was so concerned. If I did, I would be a rich man." Then he laughed.

But Mother didn't laugh. "You forget," she said, "that I am not a new mother. Having Mary Jane and Josh makes me a seasoned veteran. They also provide comparisons."

"No, no, no, no, no," he said, shaking his head. "That's just the problem. You should never compare the development of one child with another. Every child develops at its own rate. You don't want to be one of those pushy mothers now, do you?"

Mother forced a smile and shook her head.

As we left his office, I gritted my teeth and clenched my fists because I knew he was going to do it again. He did. Dr. Zefrelli called out across the room, "Now don't forget, Mary Jane, big girls are not supposed to pinch little babies." And sure enough, my face did it again—beet red!

As I remember, I chattered all the way home, but other than answering "yes" or "no" to direct questions, Mother was more than quiet; she was troubled.

Not long after our visit to Dr. Zefrelli's office we noticed that Mother began to change. She had usually been a cheerful person, but now she was often short-tempered. Sometimes, when Josh or I asked her a question, she apparently did not hear it until we asked it several times. I often saw her standing and watching Jeremiah as he slept. Sometimes she awakened him and tried to help him sit up or attract his attention with colorful toys.

And then to make things worse, Dad and Mother began to argue more frequently. It seemed that everything went wrong—dinner wasn't ready on time...the roast was overcooked...the garbage disposal started coughing...and the washing machine died. They argued about many things, but in looking back, I think most of the problem was Mother's concern about Jeremiah. That situation did not get better; instead it became worse.

The First Year

December 22—Jeremiah sat alone! What a nice Christmas gift, especially for Mother because she had worried more than the rest of us.

To make our joy complete, it snowed—eight inches of the most beautifully hazardous snow ever—and school closed two days early. After two hours of searching Josh and I finally found our sled under the back porch (where he swore he had not put it). By the evening of the first day we had a gigantic snowman in our front yard complete with a plaid scarf, a brown fedora, and charcoal buttons for eyes. He was our pride and joy and the envy of the neighborhood.

I had assumed that, because Mother had been so concerned about Jeremiah's ability to sit up, when he did everyone would live happily ever after. That wasn't the case at all. Although Mother seemed quite relieved, soon her concern was drawn to something else: Jeremiah was not crawling.

I decided that mothers were usually concerned with present problems but they quickly forgot past achievements.

I mean, after all, Jeremiah was just a baby! I couldn't see what all the fuss was about. So he didn't crawl today—big deal; he would crawl next week or next month. What was the hurry? I think maybe Dad agreed with me, but Mother acted as if these first months of Jeremiah's life were the most important.

I don't know who Josh agreed with or if he even thought about it. As I said, baseball was his life. Jeremiah would have had to have a batting average in the seven hundreds to get more than a passing nod from Josh.

Looking back, I wonder why I wasn't more aware of what was happening to Mother. Certainly the third grade wasn't so exciting that I couldn't have picked up more of the bad vibrations that were bouncing off the walls in our house. Maybe that was the trouble—the vibes weren't bouncing; they were hitting the walls with silent thuds, then oozing down the woodwork.

Perhaps another reason why Josh and I weren't completely aware of the problems at home was that Mother tried to hide them from us. When we came home from school she met us at the door with a smile on her face. So we had little idea of the torment she had known during the days.

March 25—Jeremiah's first birthday party. Even though it wasn't really a party, Mother baked a cake and we drank punch.

Let's face it—what can you do for a one-year-old kid? You can't invite his friends because he hasn't many. That first year is really restricted. There isn't such a thing as baby Scouts or a pre-toddler's bowling league.

If Jeremiah had not seen other babies in the church nursery on Sunday mornings, he might have thought that he was the only baby in the whole world. That could be enough to discourage a little kid. Right? Right. I mean, everyone he sees is taller than he is, bigger than he is, and they all talk to each other.

Jeremiah couldn't talk yet. Oh, of course, he made sounds, but no words. However, he did know his own name—or at least the sound of it. When we said "Jeremiah," he would turn and look at us and laugh his friendly laugh.

Jeremiah was like a hurt little sparrow that couldn't fly. He could move his arms and legs, but he didn't go anywhere. He could make sounds, but those sounds weren't words that we could understand. He wasn't like other brothers at all. It appeared that Jeremiah was one of a kind.

More Wait and See

Have you ever noticed that most little children are described in terms of *can?* Such as:

He *can* walk now.

He *can* say Mama and Daddy.

He *can* stack blocks.

He *can* run.

He *can* tie his own shoes.

He *can* ride a tricycle.

That wasn't the way it was with Jeremiah. We became aware that we were describing him in terms of can'ts.

He *can't* walk yet.

He *can't* talk.

He *can't* see well.

He *can't* stack blocks.

He *can't* feed himself.

In short, he couldn't do most of the things that other children his age could do.

In Jeremiah's life, the next three years might best be called the years of the "wait-and-see" specialists.

It seemed there was a specialist for each of Jeremiah's problems—an eye doctor for his eyes, an ear doctor for his ears, a bone specialist for his legs, a speech therapist to help him talk.

Jeremiah did a nifty job of confusing all of them. For instance, at first, the eye doctor thought that Jeremiah's left eye did not follow the right eye because he could not see with it. Since Jeremiah could not say which direction the E's were pointing, the doctor had to consider blindness as a possibility. But when he examined the iris and cornea, he couldn't find anything wrong with the eye. It was concluded that the eye wandered outward because the muscles were weak. Six months later when the doctor was ready to advise surgery, the eye started to move. So Mother was advised to wait a while longer and see if the condition would improve with time.

When the speech therapist first saw Jeremiah, she told Mother that the reason he did not talk was probably that the other members in the family did not set good examples for him. But after she met us and realized that we were constant talkers, she decided that maybe the problem was that Jeremiah had never been able to get a word in edgewise.

When she suspected Jeremiah was deaf, we were sent to an ear doctor for hearing tests. The ear doctor could not find anything physically wrong with my brother's ears. Jeremiah could not cooperate and answer all the questions so the doctor couldn't be sure whether he could hear well or not. However, he did think that Jeremiah could hear voices and words.

Then the speech therapist wondered if something was wrong with the formation of Jeremiah's mouth or vocal cords. When the doctor examined him, he too thought perhaps he had found the answer. The roof of Jeremiah's mouth was higher than normal and quite narrow from side to side. The next day, my little brother said, "Mama." Two days later he said, "Dada." And three days later, he said, "Milk." So it was concluded that his mouth was all right.

The orthopedist thought that corrective shoes would help straighten Jeremiah's legs and help him gain better balance. His legs did seem to straighten during the next two years, but his balance did not improve. He never walked. Instead, he moved in a half-run on his toes almost like an awkward ballet dancer.

Every six months the prescriptions for the shoes were changed, but if Jeremiah's half-run became more coordinated, it certainly was not noticeable. He still fell down a lot.

The doctors were firm believers in the "wait and see."

"These things take time," they said.

Mother said that if she had a nickel for every time she had been told to "wait and see," by now she could afford to buy New York City, Las

Vegas, and all of the state of California.

None of the specialists seemed alarmed by Jeremiah's problems, but my mother became more and more concerned because she knew that he was not getting better.

Finally, Dr. Zefrelli suggested that Jeremiah be taken to the county diagnostic clinic for a complete series of tests.

Mother agreed.

As we drove home, I asked, "What's a diagnostic clinic?"

"It's a place where they will test Jeremiah and try to find out what is wrong with him."

"But Dr. Zefrelli said that we shouldn't worry about it—that in time Jeremiah would be better."

"Dr. Zefrelli doesn't believe that anymore," Mother answered.

I started to ask another question, but when I looked up, Mother's eyes were filled with tears. I decided my question could wait.

"Hopeless"

From the outside, the County Diagnostic Clinic looked more like a school than a hospital but inside it was a toss-up. There were waiting rooms as in a hospital or a doctor's office and little tables and chairs as in grade schools. All the walls were white and the place looked clean—too clean. I knew I had better not touch anything.

I remember the day vividly. It was the Friday that a science project was supposed to be turned in. I got to skip school which meant I had a two-day extension to complete my paper-mache volcano. Mainly, I remember it because the things I heard that day were to greatly affect Jeremiah's life.

I had not gone with them the first two days of the tests. However, the results of the tests were to be given on the third day, so Mother thought that it would be a good idea if I were there to take care of Jeremiah so both she and Dad could listen carefully. As it turned out, I got to listen too, because no sooner had we entered Dr. Trask's office than Jeremiah fell asleep.

"Mr. and Mrs. Rodgers," Dr. Trask said, "after carefully considering the tests, our staff has drawn several conclusions about Jeremiah."

We waited when he paused.

"As I'm sure you are aware, Jeremiah has several problems. First, it is obvious that his coordination is far below what we would expect of a four-and-a-half-year-old. He walks on the balls of his feet and his leg muscles seem very tight."

I looked down at Jeremiah's little legs. Although I must have noticed before how thin they were, I guess I really hadn't thought much about it. They were thin and their little muscles did seem tightened even as he slept.

"We were told that orthopedic shoes would help strengthen his legs and improve his balance," Mother said.

"Yes," Dr. Trask replied, and then went on to say, "His vision is of prime concern."

My mother interrupted, "We were told to wait to have the operation because there was a chance that the eye might straighten in time."

"Yes," Dr. Trask said, again nodding his head in agreement. "That was good advice, but I think we have waited long enough. I think it is doubtful that the eye muscles will straighten without surgery."

Jeremiah stirred for a moment, then placed his

head back in my lap. How peacefully he slept while surgeon's blades were being discussed.

"All right," my father said, reaching across and placing his hand on my mother's hand. She nodded her head in agreement.

"As for Jeremiah's drooling," the doctor said, "I think that will diminish in time—after all of his adult teeth are in."

"But he drools almost constantly," my mother said.

"Yes, I know," the doctor answered.

"You mean there is nothing we can do to stop it?" my mother asked.

"I think time will help," he repeated.

I saw my mother look at the doctor with a very straight and stern expression. I had seen such a look on her face before when she was very annoyed. She started to say something, but decided to wait.

"And what about kindergarten?" my father asked. "Do you think we should wait a year to give him more time to mature?"

"No," Dr. Trask said. "I think you should consider enrolling Jeremiah in a special education kindergarten."

Suddenly my mother spoke up. "Are you saying that Jeremiah is..." she took a breath, then said the words, slowly..."mentally retarded?"

"Why, yes," Dr. Trask said, looking at my parents. "I thought you knew that."

"I think we knew," my father replied, "but no one told us. We were told to wait and see."

"No one has mentioned mental retardation before?" Dr. Trask asked.

"No one," my mother answered firmly.

"I'm sorry," the doctor said, "but I thought you were aware of why we were testing Jeremiah."

"We had hoped you would find out what's wrong with him," my father said.

"Well," the doctor replied, "we have. Your son is mentally retarded. His I.Q. is somewhere between 60 and 70. It's hard to be sure because of his limited speech and, of course, he doesn't write."

"All right," my mother said suddenly. "What can we do to make Jeremiah well?"

Dr. Trask looked at her sympathetically and said, "Mrs. Rodgers, for Jeremiah's sake, the first thing we can do is to adjust ourselves to his limitations."

"What do you mean?" she asked.

"I mean we must see Jeremiah as he really is and adjust our expectations of him. There are many things he can learn to do, and he can have a very happy life if he is not frustrated by our expecting too much from him. We must be realistic about his future and his abilities."

"What can we expect?" my father asked.

"He will probably be able to learn to dress himself, and to do simple tasks. The best thing that you can do is to give him plenty of *TLC.*"

"*TLC?*" my mother questioned. "What's that?"

"*Tender Loving Care,*" the doctor said with a smile on his face.

"Dr. Trask," my mother said, without returning a smile, "if tender loving care would make Jeremiah well, we would have no reason to talk with you, because he would have been well a long time ago."

"I didn't mean..." he started.

"We know what you mean," my mother interrupted. "It's just that we have no need for such suggestions because we love Jeremiah very much—not because he's hurt or our child or anything like that. It's simply that he is easy to love."

"Yes, of course," the doctor replied.

Suddenly my mother asked matter-of-factly, "What are Jeremiah's chances of getting well?"

"What do you mean by *well?*" the doctor asked.

"I mean normal," my mother said. "When I say *normal* I mean like M.J. and Josh and children in school!"

"It would be unrealistic to maintain such hopes," the doctor answered.

"Are you saying that it is hopeless for Jeremiah to be made well?"

"We must be realistic," he said.

"Please answer my question," my mother demanded.

"Yes," he said finally. "It is hopeless."

The silence was thunderous.

I wished I were somewhere else—anywhere; I just wanted to get out of the room because I thought Mother would start crying. I knew if she did, I would cry too. But to my surprise, there were no tears. Instead, she said to the doctor, "I don't believe that. I don't believe that Jeremiah's condition is hopeless. I think *you* believe that, but I think *you* are wrong."

"Please, Mrs. Rodgers," the doctor said, "please be reasonable."

"Don't talk to me about reason. I have been reasonable far too long. For four years I have been saying there is something wrong with Jeremiah, and during that time I was told funny stories about overly concerned mothers and was repeatedly told that in time I would laugh at how silly I had been. Well, it's been some time now, but I'm not laughing. Do you know why?"

She didn't give the doctor a chance to answer.

"I'll tell you why," Mother continued. "Because, I was not overly concerned—*I was right!* Something *was* wrong with Jeremiah—and in time he *did not* get better. You see, the truth is that for four years I have been right, and the doctors who convinced me to wait and see were wrong.

"Now then," she said, like a lawyer drawing closer to the witness, "today someone *finally* agrees that something—many things—are wrong with Jeremiah. But now you say his condition is hopeless. I say it is not. You are wrong. I am right!"

Without pausing for a breath, Mother bent down and took Jeremiah into her arms. "Come, Robert," she said to my father. "Let's go home."

My father stood up, sort of nodded his head

toward the doctor, and said to me, "Come on, M.J."

We walked straight out of the building to the parking lot. Boy, was I surprised at Mother, talking to the doctor like that. I think Dad was surprised too. In the office she had been strong and forceful—but the minute she sat down in the car all of her strength turned to tears and she cried for a long time.

I remember that Jeremiah woke up for a moment, looked around, and then leaned his head on Mother's shoulder and went back to sleep, never knowing that the tears she cried were for him.

I don't want to write anymore about it—not yet—because if I do, I will only get weepy and sloppy.

Okay, He Isn't Perfect— So What?

I don't remember the first time I heard the term "mental retardation." It may have been on television, I don't know. Anyway it did not seem important for I never thought that anyone close to our family would be mentally retarded. I couldn't imagine such a label on Jeremiah because he wasn't dumb; he just had problems—or, at least that's what we told ourselves. Maybe he didn't talk a lot and maybe he couldn't run, but he had a great smile and he was really a lovely person.

When my friends came to our house, they never said, "Oooh—what's wrong with your brother?" Instead they exclaimed, "Oh, isn't he cute!" Alice MacGregor really loved Jeremiah, and so did Sarah Attenborough. All my friends seemed to agree that Josh was a pain but Jeremiah was someone special.

43

No one seemed to mind taking the time to bend down and tie his shoes or button his shirt or pick him up. One thing for certain, Jeremiah Rodgers got more than his share of hugs. He received plenty of attention too—not only from Mother and Dad; I spent hours with him, showing him how to stack blocks and wash his hands. Even Josh sensed Jeremiah's needs. Josh was the one who taught him to catch a beach ball.

Don't get the wrong idea. It wasn't all peaches and cream or springtime and daisies. We didn't become the great all-American family overnight. Josh and I still growled at each other when we met in the hallway. And Mom and Dad's arguments didn't stop completely, but somehow we all seemed to be a little—well—more pleasant (and certainly more patient) when we were with Jeremiah.

It was simple. Because he could not button his shirt, someone had to do it for him. Since he could not get his arms into his sleeves by himself, someone had to help. Because he ate very slowly, and it was difficult for him to maneuver a spoon from his plate to his mouth, someone had to feed him. Quite often that someone was Mother, but not always; most often the person who happened to be close to Jeremiah would automatically help him. It wasn't because that person was expected to, but because that person liked him and realized that he needed help.

A Vicious Circle

I have mentioned occasions when my mother cried. I would not want to give the impression that she cried at the drop of a hat, for that was not the case. During the first five years of Jeremiah's life, those were the only three times I saw her reduced to tears. Perhaps there were tears shed in private, I do not know, but to the family Mother retained a quiet strength and most of the time she maintained a good sense of humor.

She was the first one up in the morning and the last in bed at night. She has said many times that to be a housewife and mother, a woman must wear many hats—she is a housekeeper, a maid, a cook, a laundress, an accountant, a supplies officer, a drill sergeant, a nurse, a nutritionist, a chauffeur, a playground supervisor, an answerer of a thousand and one questions, a good listener, a commander, and a friend. I think Mother managed all of those things rather well.

Maybe it was because of Jeremiah's problems and the fact that he required more attention than other kids, but as a family we began to notice each other more than most family members do. I became aware that Mother worked long hours and rarely had time to sit down. Although we never discussed it, I think Josh must have sensed it too because he played with Jeremiah for long periods of time.

For Jeremiah, play was a big problem. He could not play with children his own age. He could not understand the rules of their games, and they would quickly become impatient with him and run off to another yard to play. Since Jeremiah couldn't run more than fifteen feet before stumbling or falling, it was easy for them to leave him far behind.

It became clear to us that if Jeremiah were going to have anyone to play with, it would have to be us.

"It's a vicious circle," Mother said one day as she stopped to watch some children play across the street.

"What do you mean?" I asked.

"I mean," she answered, "because Jeremiah does not understand the games they play, they will not play with him, and because they will not play with him, he doesn't have a chance to learn their games."

"They're just little creeps," I said in disgust.

46

"No, M.J., it isn't their fault that Jeremiah can't keep up with them," Mother explained. "You see, there is no way that we can slow down all other children to wait for Jeremiah. What we must do is find a way to speed up Jeremiah."

"But how can we do that?" I asked.

"I don't know," Mother said. "I don't know."

The Gaping Gawkers and the Turning Yackers

I have heard that some families with children who don't appear to be normal—such as children who have huge birthmarks, clubfeet, a harelip, or some other disfigurement, or some who are considered "mentally retarded"—deliberately keep these children at home. They don't take them out shopping because of the curiosity of other people.

We tried to take Jeremiah as many places as we could. Mother said that if we didn't take him to the supermarket or to a shopping center he would never know what those were.

We were not ashamed of Jeremiah. On the contrary, we were quite proud of him. A lot of kids can just stand up and walk with little or no effort. Right? Right! But Jeremiah couldn't walk without a lot of effort and concentration. It was the same with eating. Other kids his age could cram in the food faster than a stoker can shovel coal into a furnace, but it was difficult for Jeremiah. It was hard for him to fill his spoon and bring it to his mouth without spilling it. While other kids gobbled down their food, Jeremiah chewed very slowly. And take stacking blocks. Most kids could stack a tower of blocks in hardly any time and with one quick push could bring them tumbling down. For Jeremiah, the placement of each block required his full attention.

Which children should be most admired—those kids who can do everything so effortlessly or those kids who have to work so hard to accomplish even the simplest of tasks?

When we looked at it properly, it became quite simple. For Jeremiah to run all the way across our front yard without falling down was equivalent to an Olympic runner's winning a race because both required the best efforts from each of them.

For Jeremiah to feed himself required the patience and concentration of a diamond cutter.

For Jeremiah to stack blocks required the precision of a man driving a derrick.

When one looked at Jeremiah and saw what he accomplished in spite of his handicaps, it became obvious why we were proud of him and admired him. However, those who did not have the opportunity to see his accomplishments seemed to see only his problems.

Although we learned to expect people to look at Jeremiah with curiosity, we never really grew accustomed to it. Most often we pretended that we didn't see them, but sometimes it was impossible to ignore them. There were several species of curious lookers. Josh and I labeled some of them.

The Peeking Sidewinders. These people didn't turn their heads to look; they peeked out of the corner of their eyes. That was dangerous for them; sometimes they bumped into other people or into grocery carts. In a department store one woman walked straight into a solid wall. Served her right.

The Snooty Sneakers. We called them sneakers because they tried not to be seen looking at us from behind shelves, posts, or another person. We called them snooty because Mother told Josh and me not to use the word *snotty*. Anyway, the Snooty Sneakers were always putting handkerchiefs to their noses and seemed to sniff a lot.

The Gaping Gawkers. These people stood with their mouths wide open and looked. They came in all heights, weights, and mouth sizes.

The Turning Yackers. There were lookers who turned to someone standing nearby and said, "Don't look now but..." Immediately the other person turned and looked. Then they all began to yak, yak, yak.

The Stalking Starers. These people followed us through the store, staring. Mother told us to ignore them. Most of the time Josh and I pretended we did, but sometimes after we had enough we would quietly turn toward one of them, cross our eyes, and stick out our tongues.

The Old Perfectly Frankers. These were usually older women with blue-tinted hair who seemed to feel they had lived long enough to be rude if and when they wished. They looked down their noses at boys with long hair and girls in faded jeans. In our case they walked straight up to us and said, "What on earth is the matter with that child?" Their voices were usually loud. Maybe that was because they were often hard of hearing which meant that any answer given to them had to be almost shouted too.

The Poor Things. These were the ones who looked, shook their heads, said, "Poor thing," and went on their way.

The Pretending Passersby. They walked right by, or even stood and talked with us about other things, while pretending they did not see Jeremiah or, at least, any of his obvious problems. They meant well.

Of course, there were mixtures of these species. There were *the Stalking Sneakers, the Peeking Poor Things, the Sneaking Gawkers, the Gaping Frankers,* and *the Pretending Sidewinders.*

I am sure that some of these people's actions appeared worse to us than they really were because, even though we tried not to be, we were probably overly sensitive. I think we were most afraid that Jeremiah might sometimes notice them and realize that people were looking at him strangely. Perhaps some of these people did not mean to be rude. There is the possibility that some were sincerely concerned and wished they could someway be of help. But whatever their reasons, we either had to endure their looks or keep Jeremiah at home. We preferred to endure their looks.

Charlie

It was difficult for us to fully understand Jeremiah's reactions because of his lack of reactions. That sounds confusing because it was confusing.

We learned to understand the extremes of Jeremiah's reactions. For instance, when he cried we knew that he didn't like something or he didn't want to do something. When he laughed we knew that he was enjoying something or something appeared to be funny to him. But we weren't always sure why he was upset or why he was amused.

Neither could we always predict what things would make him laugh or what things would frighten him. We learned that some toys which made sudden loud noises scared him; he would hide from them or run to one of us and cover his ears. He liked to go for a ride in the car, but if a horn was honked nearby he would curl up in the seat like a frightened little animal. The sounds of police car or ambulance sirens would cause him to scream in terror.

Jeremiah had no fear of heights. Although his balance was not good, if one of us did not constantly hold on to him he would run ahead of us in department stores and charge down a stairway or an escalator.

He loved animals. I think he would have run up to a tiger or a lion and petted it. If he saw a dog, no matter how big it was, he would say, "Cute dog," and run straight toward it.

Sometimes when Mom or Dad scolded him he would laugh. At other times when they started to pick him up to hug him, he would start crying.

He did not like taking a bath in the tub—the sound of the shower frightened him—but at the swimming pool he would jump in the deep water even though he couldn't swim.

Obviously, he was a strange little kid and, just as obviously, a lot of time was required to watch him and take care of him.

Dad once said, "Jeremiah is a twenty-four-hour-a-day Chinese puzzle."

I think he was right, because no matter how hard we tried to figure out why Jeremiah acted so strangely, we simply couldn't fit all the pieces together. At the same time, this little riddle of a kid could be so loving and so sweet that we couldn't help but love him more.

Some mornings he would come into my room,

climb up on my bed, and say, "Wake up, it's Christmas."

"It's not Christmas yet," I'd say.

"Not yet—someday."

"That's right," I would answer. "Christmas is in December."

"December," he would repeat.

The next morning he might do the same thing all over, and again he would respond to December as if it were a new word that he had never heard before.

One morning he came running into my room.

"Wake up," he demanded. "Wake up." "See dog," he said, excitedly. "See dog!"

"There isn't a dog in here," I told him.

"Outside. Come see!"

He kept pulling me until finally I got out of my bed and, sleepy-eyed though I was, I followed him into his room.

"See dog," he said.

"There's no . . . dog," I started to say but when I looked at the window where he was pointing, I saw a red squirrel sitting on the window ledge looking in at us. If the squirrel was afraid of us, he certainly didn't show it. He sat there and watched us as we walked to the window.

"My dog," Jeremiah announced.

"No," I laughed. "That's not a dog."

"Dog," he repeated.

"No, It's a squirrel."

"No," he insisted.

I walked over to the bookcase, took down a

book, opened it to a colorful picture of a squirrel, and said, "Look, it's a squirrel. It says so in the book."

Jeremiah looked at the picture carefully, then at the furry animal on the window ledge, and back at the book again. Then, as if he refused to admit he had been wrong, he changed the subject.

"Name?" he asked.

"Squirrel," I answered.

"No," he said. "Name?"

Finally realizing what he meant, I answered, "He doesn't have a name."

"Does too," he said. "M.J., guess."

"Okay," I said sitting down. "Is his name Tom?"

"No," Jeremiah answered, shaking his head.

"Is it Jim?"

"No."

"What is it then?" I asked.

He looked at me smugly, as if to let me know he knew something that I did not. "Charlie," he said.

"How do you know that?" I asked.

"He told me," he answered.

Of course that ended the argument. How could I argue with Jeremiah if the squirrel had told him?

From that time on we called the squirrel Charlie, and the squirrel didn't seem to mind. In the mornings he often came to the window ledge and looked in at us. In return for the pleasure of his company, we left bread scraps for him. For three or four months we saw Charlie every day. Then one morning he didn't show up.

"Where's Charlie?" Jeremiah wanted to know.

Mother thought quicker than I did and answered, "Maybe he went home to his mother."

"No," Jeremiah said. "He got married."

No one knew for sure what happened to Charlie. Josh said that the neighbor's cat had him for dinner. (Boys can be so disgusting.) I preferred to think that Jeremiah was right and imagined Charlie cozy and warm in a nest inside some hollow oak tree.

Every once in a while a squirrel scurried across our backyard and Jeremiah ran to the window and waved. Sometimes when we were riding in the car, he'd see a red squirrel and call out, "Hi, Charlie."

"If that's Charlie," Josh said one time, "then why doesn't he still come to see you?"

I thought, *Oh boy, here come the tears,* but Jeremiah answered, "He's busy."

"How do you know?" Josh went on to question.

"Charlie told me," Jeremiah said, again ending the conversation.

The Five-year-old Drop-out

When Jeremiah was five years old, he was enrolled in a special education class instead of kindergarten.

"It's for the best that he be with children like himself," Mother was told.

Each morning she took him to the school. As he walked toward the door, she watched the other children on the playground turn and look at him. Sometimes they whispered, sometimes their voices were louder and she heard the words "mentally retarded." Although she tried to ignore these things, she couldn't. She could clearly see that Jeremiah was fast becoming a third-class citizen.

After visiting the classroom one day, she came home even more upset than usual.

"I will not let Jeremiah go back to that class," she told my father.

"Why not?" he asked.

"Because it is filled with hopeless children. If he stays in that class, he will get worse instead of better."

"Aren't the teachers good?" Dad asked.

"Very nice," she answered.

"Aren't the rooms clean?"

"Very clean," she said.

"Then why?"

"Because they're *special*," she told him. "I don't want Jeremiah in a *special* world."

Mother sat down. "You see, I think Jeremiah is much better than he might have been because he has had the advantage of being with M.J. and Josh. He has learned much from them. Most of the children I saw in the special class are in as bad a condition as Jeremiah and some of them are worse."

"That's why they have those classes," Dad said.

"I know," Mother replied. "But don't you see? If Jeremiah stays in there, then most of the people he knows will be *special*. You know how he mimics things he sees and copies things other people do. If he stays in that class he will become more and more like his classmates and less and less like everyday people.

"Those special classrooms are like cages," she said, "nice, neat cages. They are clean and the children are cared for, but I don't want Jeremiah that safe and that cared for. I want him outside where the action is. The teacher told me this morning that she works very hard to keep the children from becoming frustrated. I want

Jeremiah to have a chance to be frustrated like everyone else.

"If he stays in that special class, then we will have to build a special world for him to live in for the rest of his life. I don't know how to do that."

"So what do we do?" Dad said, thinking aloud.

"Since we don't know how to change the world, we have to find a way to change Jeremiah," Mother reasoned.

So Jeremiah became a five-year-old drop-out. He did not return to school the following week.

Not long after that Mother noticed a book in a bookstore. It had a fascinating title, *How to Teach Your Baby to Read*. At first Mother thought the author really meant "child" instead of "baby," but when she glanced through the pages she saw that the author really believed babies can be taught to read. Mother decided if babies could learn to read, there was no reason she could not teach Jeremiah. She bought the book.

It's funny how a person buys something for one reason and later finds that it is more useful for another reason.

When Mother read the book she learned that its author, Glenn Doman, was not a teacher as she had supposed. Instead, he was a physical therapist and director of a place in Philadelphia, Pennsylvania, called The Institutes for the Achievement of Human Potential. Mr. Doman and a staff of medical doctors, educators, and physical therapists had created therapy programs for brain-injured children. "The goal of The Institutes' staff members," Mr. Doman wrote, "is for each and every child to get well."

That had been Mother's goal for Jeremiah!

Then a strange thing happened. After reading the book, Mother was afraid to try to teach Jeremiah to read. She was afraid that he might not learn and she would become even more discouraged. While mothers of normal children feel free to try almost anything with their children, mothers of hurt children become afraid that they will do something wrong. These mothers question almost everything they do.

That was a terrible time for Mother.

A Call to Order

"There will be a family meeting tonight," Mother announced to Josh and me when we arrived home from school one afternoon.

"What's wrong?" I asked.

"Nothing's wrong," Mother said. "We have something important to discuss."

"Something important," I said to myself as I hurried to my room. "I bet..."

I surveyed the condition of my room. On a zero to ten neatness scale, I quickly evaluated that my room would score about eight and one-half which was most certainly at least three points above the necessity to call an assembly of all troops for inspection.

I decided that if it wasn't my room that was in question, then it must be Josh's. I ran across the hall and opened his door.

"You're supposed to knock," Josh growled.

"It's an emergency," I explained. I looked about

quickly. His room scored a doubtful seven, but at least a six was well above a court martial or public disgrace.

"What do you mean—*emergency?*" Josh questioned as one would speak to a spy from the enemy's camp.

"It's not our rooms," I said. "Have you done anything in the last three days that would make Mom and Dad call a family meeting?"

"None of your business," he answered.

"Thanks, Josh, you're a gentleman to your grubby fingernails and your tennis shoes stink," I retorted, giving tit-for-tat—which is the only way one can communicate with a baseball freak. I exited.

A few minutes later Josh *knocked* at the door to my room (a pointed example if there ever was one).

"Come in," I said in mock friendliness, returning his courtesy.

Josh stepped inside.

"I haven't done anything to get in trouble," he said. "I thought maybe *you* had done something."

"Not that I know of," I told him.

"Maybe it has something to do with our vacation," he suggested.

"That's it," I agreed. "I bet we're going to vote on where we want to go."

As it turned out, that piece of splendid deduction was at least half right. We were going to discuss our family vacation time but not necessarily a vacation.

Our family meetings were held with both the formality and the flourish of a court trial. Dad got the idea from either a Brady Bunch television show or the old Clifton Webb movie, *Cheaper by the Dozen*. It looked great with seven or twelve kids sitting in a drawing room discussing and debating issues in parliamentary order with their parents. Somehow it wasn't quite the same with only five people at the kitchen table.

"The meeting is called to order," my father said as always, tapping a spoon on the tabletop.

"I've called a family meeting tonight to discuss a most important matter which requires our utmost consideration," Dad began. "As all of us are aware, we have vacation time in July. To date it has been suggested that we plan to:

"*One*—visit Disneyland,

"*Two*—camp in the Rockies,

"*Three*—float on the River of No Return [my suggestion],

"*Four*—see a doubleheader at the Houston Astrodome [Josh's],

"*Five*—fish on a nearby lake [Dad's], or

"*Six*—stay home and paint the house [obviously that was Mom's].

"Your mother now has another suggestion which, as you will see, demands that we discuss and consider it most carefully. The chair recognizes Mrs. Rodgers." (Dad really overdid it—"The chair recognizes Mrs. Rodgers"—now really!)

"Thank you," said Mrs. Rodgers (our mother) to the Chair (our father), going along with the inflicted order of pomp and circumstance. Then she turned toward those assembled (Josh, Jeremiah, and me).

"As we know, everything is not well with one member of our family," Mother said, nodding toward Jeremiah. "It is obvious that Jeremiah has a great many problems. It now appears that time is not going to heal whatever is wrong—and it should be clear that we are not going to find someone with a magic wand who can make his ailments disappear. In fact, although we don't like to admit it, we realize that Jeremiah's condition is getting worse instead of better because he is falling farther and farther behind children his own age. If we do not find a way to make Jeremiah better, then it looks as if someone will have to take care of him for the rest of his life."

"Don't worry about that," I quickly offered. "We love Jeremiah. We don't mind taking care of him."

"We like to," Josh added.

Jeremiah laughed and said, "Me, too."

Mother smiled, then continued. "Both of you have been a great deal of help and I know you both love Jeremiah—but I don't think either of you realizes what it will mean if his condition does not improve. It's fun to play with him now because he is little and cute. Because it is easy to pick him up and cuddle him, we do not see him as being a chore; but as he gets older he will get taller and heavier, and if what they told us at the clinic proves to be true, Jeremiah will have to be cared for as one would care for a child for the rest of his life. It makes me proud of both of you to think that you are willing to help in his care, but I think we have to think of what's best for him."

I held my breath. I thought for a moment that Mom and Dad were about to suggest that Jeremiah be placed in an institution somewhere. I couldn't believe such a thing. I looked at Josh and saw the same fears cross his mind.

"As you both know," Mother continued, "the staff at the clinic has told us that Jeremiah's condition cannot be improved and that it would be foolish for us to maintain the hope that he could ever be made well."

Mother patted my dad's hand. "Your father and I choose to be foolish; we refuse to give up such a hope."

"I do too," I said quickly.

Josh agreed.

"Well, then," Mother smiled, "it looks like we're nothing but a family of fools."

We laughed.

And Jeremiah laughed.

"A few months ago," Mother said, becoming serious again, "your father and I heard about a place in Philadelphia called The Institutes for the Achievement of Human Potential. It seems that they have developed new methods of therapy for so-called "mentally retarded" children. At The Institutes they teach parents how to do these therapy programs with their child. Their programs are very demanding and often take

66

many hours every day. If there is any hope that we can make Jeremiah well, your father and I think it must be at this place."

"Let's take Jeremiah there!" Josh exclaimed.

"Well, that's why we called this meeting," my father said. "We have an appointment for Jeremiah on the twentieth of July, which poses some problems."

"Such as?" I asked.

"Such as time and money. Let's discuss time first," he said. "Since we are required to be in Philadelphia for five days, that would take care of one week of our vacation."

Josh and I got the idea.

"But we still have another week," I said.

"Yes, that's true," Dad replied. "However, if we place Jeremiah on this program of therapy, we will have to take him back to Philadelphia once every six months, which means that we would need to save every dollar and every penny we can get hold of."

"So," Mother said, "the question is, do we take Jeremiah to Philadelphia or do we have a vacation?"

Everyone became quiet, even Jeremiah. He just sat there looking at us.

"Well," Josh said, "the Astrodome will still be there next year. Let's get Jeremiah fixed up this year."

I was proud of Josh.

"I vote for Philadelphia, too," I said.

"So do I," said Mother.

"Aye," said the Chairman of the Board.

"Me, too," said Jeremiah, suddenly laughing.

"That makes it unanimous," my father said, tapping the spoon on the table. "Meeting adjourned."

"Switches On"

From Indianapolis, Indiana, to Philadelphia, Pennsylvania, is 824 miles—two hours on a jet plane; sixteen hours by car; one long, long tedious day of driving; or two semi-long, tedious days. We decided to take the semi-long, two-day excursion, allowing one day to rest before Jeremiah's appointment.

I sat looking out the car window watching the green fields float by, touched by the summer sun. I realized that our trip could not be considered as mere distance composed of miles; my family had embarked upon a journey into the unknown. Our mission was not to discover what the Ohio and Pennsylvania countryside looked like; ours was a pilgrimage of greater importance. Our objective was to find out what was wrong with Jeremiah and to learn if he could be fixed.

69

As I rode along, I began to imagine what The Institutes might be like. I pictured in my mind a scientist's laboratory with huge metal coils spiraling to the ceiling—hissing bolts of electricity flashing like lightning shooting out from one coil to another. In the center of the room I saw a giant microscope aimed at the operating table below. The doors opened; the doctors and nurses, dressed in white, entered. They walked to the table in somber silence. I saw my little brother Jeremiah lying on the table.

"Switches on," the doctor commanded in a voice that was faintly familiar.

"Switches on," echoed the voice of the nurse.

A hand reached for the control panel. With precision, it pulled the levers—one, two, three, four, five, six, seven; all switches were turned on.

"Switches on," the operator reported in a loud, clear voice.

"Switches on," echoed the nurse.

"Open lens," commanded the doctor. (I finally recognized his voice, it was a cross between Boris Karloff's and James Mason's.)

"Open lens," repeated the nurse.

The operator removed the lens cap from the giant microscope.

"Lens opened," he reported.

"Lens opened," said the nurse.

"Focus," ordered the doctor.

"Focus," repeated the nurse.

The operator's hand took hold of the controls; the groaning sound of a powerful engine was heard as the column of the giant microscope began to move. I saw the lens move closer to Jeremiah's head as he lay quietly on the table. On one wall an enormous television screen lit up. On the screen Jeremiah's head came into view—one hundred, perhaps a thousand times larger than actual size.

The lens edged closer still.

Jeremiah's hair follicles were magnified and projected on the screen. Then one molecule of his skin filled the expanse of the lighted square.

Suddenly the screen went black.

"What happened?" I wondered. Perhaps something broke. Suddenly tiny lights appeared on the screen like distant stars. At first I didn't understand what they were. Then all at once I realized I was no longer viewing the outside of Jeremiah's head, but the giant microscope with its X-ray vision was probing inside. I was seeing a section of Jeremiah's brain; those little lights were brain cells.

"Contact!" the doctor commanded.

"Contact!" repeated the nurse.

"Hey, when are we going to stop?" a voice called out.

"In a little while," was the answer.

"But I'm hungry," the voice moaned in more familiar tones.

71

Not One of a Kind

The first thing we learned at The Institutes was that Jeremiah was not one of a kind. After seeing the thirty-two other children who were there that day, we realized that he was one of a group.

The second thing we learned was that Jeremiah's condition was better than that of many of the others being evaluated. On the other hand, some were in better condition than he was. Jeremiah was somewhere in between.

Two of the children were in wheelchairs. One could move his arms but not his legs. The other could move only his head.

Some of the children couldn't talk plainly and some couldn't talk at all.

The ones whose conditions were worse than Jeremiah's encouraged us, because we felt that if The Institutes' methods of therapy could help them, then surely Jeremiah could be helped.

However, the children who appeared better than Jeremiah frightened us a little, because we were afraid that these methods might help only them.

Another thing we noticed at The Institutes was that not all the children were from the United States. Of the thirty-two, two were from France, one was from Spain, one from Japan, two from Italy, two from Great Britain, one from Ireland, and one from Israel. We learned that twenty-two American families came from sixteen states.

After talking to some of the other people and hearing their reasons for bringing their children to The Institutes, we became aware that all these parents had been told that their child's condition was hopeless. Thirty-two hopeless children—this was hard to imagine, because the parents weren't sitting around sad-faced. Instead they were talking with each other and sometimes even laughing. The reason for their cheerfulness became clear. Like us, rather than give up they had chosen to dream, to wish, to hope.

"This room is filled with determined people," my mother said. "Or perhaps we are all fools."

As she said that I looked up and saw Jeremiah walking across the room with Josh holding tightly to his brother's hand. He looked rather confused by the sights and sounds around him.

I thought of something Mother had said long before: "I know that somewhere inside Jeremiah is a beautiful, well child wanting to be released. It is as if the real Jeremiah is held captive inside a body that he cannot control. If we can find the key that will unlock his problems, the real Jeremiah will come out for the whole world to see."

I hoped—oh how I hoped—that in this place we would find the key.

Questions and Answers

As we waited, several of the other children's names were called. With their parents they followed staff members into their offices.

Finally, a woman stepped into the waiting room and called Jeremiah's name.

As we walked toward her, she smiled. "Are you the Rodgers?" she asked.

My parents answered, "Yes."

"Welcome," she said, "My name is Gretchen Kerr. If you will follow me to my office, we'll begin to find out about Jeremiah."

"We have two other children with us," my father told her, pointing toward Josh and me.

"If they like, they are welcome to come with us or they may wait here," Ms. Kerr replied. "However, if they come with us, they must realize that we will be concentrating on Jeremiah. Most of the time they must sit quietly and listen."

She looked toward Josh and me and smiled. "That's the way it is, kids. Sorry. But it's going to take all the energy and all the concentration that we can muster to find out what's wrong with your brother."

Josh and I smiled our understanding smiles and said, "We'll be quiet."

We followed Mom and Dad into Ms. Kerr's office.

Gretchen Kerr was a tall, athletic woman who maintained, for the most part, a very down-to-business manner. However, every so often she smiled, revealing an extremely warm and friendly person.

She began, "Today the staff will ask you a lot of questions and we will examine Jeremiah both physically and medically. If during the course of the day you have any questions, you are welcome to ask them. Don't hesitate."

"I have a question now," Mother said.

"What is it?"

"How soon will we be told if Jeremiah can be made better by your therapy?"

"This evening," Ms. Kerr answered matter-of-factly. "What you will be told is whether or not we believe Jeremiah is brain-injured and if we will accept him as a candidate for one of our programs of therapy."

"Do you mean that if he is brain-injured, you won't give us a program?" Mother inquired.

"Oh, no," Ms. Kerr answered. "It's just the opposite. Brain-injured kids are the reason we are here."

"We usually find three kinds of kids," she said. "There are children who have deficient brains. For some unknown reason their brains are not formed right. As far as we know, there is nothing that we can do for these children. But, happily, we have found that there are very few of them."

"Those in the second group have psychotic brains. Their brains appear to be perfectly normal in every way, but their behavior is extremely strange. We know of nothing that we can do for these kids either. But we have found that they also are rare."

I noticed that Mother and Dad were troubled by what Ms. Kerr said about children who have psychotic brains. I was worried by that too because so often Jeremiah reacted strangely. Had we come all this way for nothing, I wondered?

"The third kind of kid we see at The Institutes," Ms. Kerr told us, "is the brain-injured child. I can tell you right now there are plenty of these. Their brains develop normally following conception, but sometime either before, during, or after birth, their brains are injured in some way."

"But which is Jeremiah?" Mother asked anxiously.

"That's what we intend to discover today," Ms. Kerr answered. "We will evaluate Jeremiah and decide if we think he has a deficient brain, a psychotic brain, or an injured brain. If our findings indicate that his brain is either deficient or psychotic, we will tell you this evening.

"However," she continued, "if we find that Jeremiah is brain-injured, then *you* have a decision to make tonight. You will need to decide if you want to come back for the next four days or not."

"We would come back, of course," Mother said quickly.

"If that's what you decide, that will be fine," Ms. Kerr replied. "However, if you do not choose to return, that will be fine too. We feel that it should be your choice."

"Are you trying to talk us out of coming back?" Dad asked abruptly.

"I certainly am not," Ms. Kerr replied. On the other hand, not one staff member here would ever try to convince you to come back if you did not choose to. You see, Mr. and Mrs. Rodgers, if we determine that Jeremiah is brain-injured, then more than likely the program of therapy which we will prescribe will be extremely demanding, not only for Jeremiah but for the whole family."

Ms. Kerr leaned forward. "Look, Mr. and Mrs. Rodgers," she said, "it is usually a very hard program. One that must be done every day—Monday, Tuesday, Wednesday, Thanksgiving, Christmas, the Fourth of July—every day. Even if you do decide to place Jeremiah on such a program, there is no guarantee that he will be made completely well."

"Has any child on one of these programs ever

gotten well?" Mother asked.

"Oh, of course," Ms. Kerr answered. "Many of our kids are now in regular schools. Some of them even become superior to so-called normal kids."

"Are there certain kinds of children that these programs can help more than others?" Dad asked.

Ms. Kerr looked up. "Do you mean can we predict which children can make it and which ones can't?"

"Not exactly," Dad replied. "What I mean is, are there certain types which are usually more successful?"

"No," Ms. Kerr answered. "We have seen completely paralyzed kids make it all the way. We have seen kids who have been labeled cerebral palsied make it all the way. We have seen kids who have been labeled mentally retarded make it all the way. And we have seen kids who have minor learning problems make it all the way into regular classrooms. On the other hand, we have also seen every one of those types fail."

"Why do they fail?" Mother asked.

"We don't always know," Ms. Kerr answered. "Some fail because the parents tire of doing the program before the child is well. Some fail because we are not smart enough to make them well. But I will make a deal with you, Mr. and Mrs. Rodgers. If you do decide to place Jeremiah on a program and he doesn't get better, no one at The Institutes will ever try to blame Jeremiah for the failure if *you* will never place the blame on him. If we are not smart enough to tell you the right things to do, then, more than likely, members of the staff will blame themselves. And we will expect the same consideration from you. If, for some reason, you do not do the program as you are instructed, then you must not try to blame anyone else for its not being done."

"Fair enough," my father said.

"Now then," Ms. Kerr said, opening a large folder, "it's my turn to ask questions. As you'll soon see, I have many to ask. It's going to be a long day."

We soon learned that she was right; it was a long day and she did have many questions. She asked pages and pages of questions and wrote all the answers that my parents gave her on the pages of the folder.

She asked about the condition of my mother's health during the time she was pregnant with Jeremiah. She asked many questions about how and when Jeremiah was born. What was his weight at the time of birth? His length? How did he look?

Every time Josh and I thought she was about to run out of questions, Ms. Kerr turned another page and asked more.

Each year of Jeremiah's life was reviewed in detail—each and every pound he gained—every inch he grew. At what age did he turn over for the first time? When did he first sit alone? Who first noticed that he had a problem? What did the doctor say?

For over two hours the questions were poured out and answers were returned. It was almost like reliving Jeremiah's life.

During most of the time, Josh and I listened. Although we grew tired of sitting quietly, we found most of the discussion interesting.

"Believe it or not," Ms. Kerr finally said, "I am out of pages, which means I have no more questions—at this time."

All of us gave big sighs of relief.

Ms. Kerr smiled. "Your day has just begun. You'll see. There will be many more questions. Jeremiah will be examined and carefully evaluated. I wish you the best of luck," she said.

She told us to go back to the waiting room until the next staff member could see us.

So...we waited.

Not Really Okay

During the course of the day, Josh and I were in many offices with Jeremiah and my parents. Although their main concern was for our little brother, the staff members all took time to visit briefly with us. From room to room the conversations we had with these people were pretty much the same.

Actually it wasn't the exciting interchange of ideas and conversations of which books are supposed to be composed but rather the kind of pleasant talk that makes one feel welcome and not like a bump on a log.

"And are you Jeremiah's sister?"

I would answer "Yes," and tell them that my name was M.J. And Josh told them his name.

"I am in the seventh grade (me)."
"I am in the sixth grade (Josh)."
"Yes, we are from Indianapolis."
"Yes, we had a nice trip."

Now, I don't intend to bore you with such trivia throughout the book. I will tell only of the things which are important and which will give you the reader a clue to what is wrong with Jeremiah.

"Clue" is really a good word here because it makes the story sound like a mystery--which, of course, it is. It's the JEREMIAH RODGERS CASE.

If you read the clues very carefully, perhaps you might find out what's wrong with Jeremiah and solve the mystery for yourself.

Now then, on with the story—

Jeremiah must have liked Mrs. Tyson the minute he saw her because he walked straight to her desk and said, "Hi."

I wasn't surprised that he liked her. Mrs. Tyson had one of those infectious smiles which began immediately when she saw us and it never seemed to find a stopping place.

"Good morning," she said to Jeremiah.

"Good morning," he repeated.

As we sat down, Jeremiah walked over to the window.

"Look," he said, pointing outside at a red squirrel that was perched on a tree limb. "There's Charlie. Hi, Charlie," he called out.

We laughed.

"No, that's not Charlie," Mother told him. "He just looks like Charlie."

"*Is* Charlie!" Jeremiah insisted.

"Is Charlie a pet?" Mrs. Tyson asked.

"He's a squirrel that used to live in our backyard," Josh told her.

"See Charlie!" Jeremiah said, turning toward us.

"That is not Charlie," Josh said firmly.

"*Is* too," Jeremiah argued.

"Charlie is in Indianapolis," I tried to explain.

"No!" Jeremiah shook his head stubbornly. "Charlie not Indypolis. Charlie *here!*"

"That's all right," Mrs. Tyson said, bending down beside him. "If you say that's Charlie, it's good enough for me."

Jeremiah smiled smugly at us and turned back to his newfound ally.

"Charlie *here!*" he said.

"Do you know what Charlie is doing?" Mrs. Tyson asked.

"Play," Jeremiah answered.

"Sometimes," Mrs. Tyson said, "but look what he has in his hands. He has an acorn. All summer long squirrels gather nuts and store them inside a tree. When winter comes they can stay inside the tree where it is nice and warm and have plenty to eat."

"Charlie's hungry," Jeremiah agreed.

"Jeremiah," Mrs. Tyson urged him, "would you like to come over by my desk and play a game?"

"No," he answered.

"I have some toys over here," she said.

He didn't even turn around to see what she had.

"Look," he finally said, pointing outside again, "Charlie's gone."

Mrs. Tyson looked out the window. "Oh, that's right," she said, seeing the empty branch. "Where do you suppose he went?" she asked.

"The bathroom," Jeremiah answered.

We laughed.

Then Jeremiah laughed too.

"If you say so," Mrs. Tyson said, smiling. "Now, why don't you come over here and let's play a game?"

Taking hold of his hand, she led him to her desk. She opened a drawer and took out some things. "Look what I have here," she said, holding them out one at a time for him to see. "A marble...a little block of wood...and a nickel."

"Look what I'm going to do with them," she told him.

"I'm going to put them inside this cloth bag. See, here they go. One. Two. Three."

Jeremiah watched as the objects were dropped into the bag.

"Now, then," she said, "what I would like for you to do is reach your hand inside and bring out the marble."

"Okay," Jeremiah said, reaching his hand inside.

In my mind's eye, I pictured the things she had dropped in the bag. To me, they were as different from each other as night is from day. Without the slightest hesitation, I could have felt the difference between the objects and brought out the one she requested.

We watched as Jeremiah's hand searched for the marble.

I could feel beads of perspiration form on my forehead. I wanted to run over to him and help him. Dad, Mom, and Josh must have felt the same way.

When his hand came out, we could see that Jeremiah hadn't found the marble. Instead, he held up the block of wood.

"Okay," Mrs. Tyson said, patting his head.

But it really wasn't *okay*.

I looked over at my parents. I could see them forcing smiles, trying to hide their concern.

You'll Be Told Tonight

We were in Sandra Brown's office.

"Mrs. Rodgers," Ms. Brown said, looking up from Jeremiah's folder, "I notice that your doctor was not sure whether or not Jeremiah has a hearing problem."

"That's right," Mother answered, "because Jeremiah couldn't cooperate in the tests."

"Yes, of course," Ms. Brown agreed. "Now then, let me ask you a question. Do *you* think Jeremiah has a hearing problem?"

"Well, I'm not absolutely sure."

"Oh, you don't have to *prove* whether he does or not; I'm asking only for your opinion."

Mother thought about it carefully, then answered. "At times I don't think he hears what I say to him. But sometimes I think he understands more than he appears to."

"I'm sure he does," Ms. Brown said.

"But there are times," Mother continued, "when I don't think he hears what has been said."

Mother looked down for a moment. "Maybe you think I'm crazy, and maybe I am. I wouldn't be surprised if I were crazy. From the time Jeremiah was born I have done little else but worry about him. At the clinic they said he is mentally retarded and that he will never be better, and when we refused to give up hope they thought we were being *unreasonable.*"

She looked up. "Maybe we are unreasonable. I don't know. But one thing I'm sure of: As sure as I'm sitting here my little boy is not dumb and he is not stupid. I know that. You asked me what I think, so I'll tell you. I think that Jeremiah is a bright little boy, but there is some kind of short circuit in his brain."

Ms. Brown nodded her head. "I couldn't agree with you more," she said.

"You're not just saying that, are you?" Mother asked quickly.

"Of course not," Ms. Brown answered. "After reviewing your answers to our questions and from the things you have told me, I think you see Jeremiah's problems quite clearly and quite realistically. But this doesn't surprise me, Mrs. Rodgers, because we have found that mothers are darned good evaluators of their children. As you said earlier today, time after time your opinion of Jeremiah's condition was right."

My father spoke up. "Are you saying that Jeremiah is brain-injured?"

"No. That is not what I'm saying," Ms. Brown answered. "At the same time, I am not saying that he is not brain-injured. What I am saying is that I think you have good opinions of Jeremiah's problems."

"Ms. Brown, when are we going to be told whether or not Jeremiah is brain-injured?" Mother asked.

"Tonight," she answered. "Now, let's see if we can find out how well this boy of yours can hear," she said, turning toward Jeremiah.

In the minutes that followed, Ms. Brown made a lot of noises with many different kinds of gadgets. Some of the sounds were loud and some were as soft as whispers. She made notes of Jeremiah's responses on the pages she had added to his folder.

"Don't Cry or I'll Cry Too"

Dr. Evan Thomas was the tallest man Jeremiah had ever seen. Jeremiah looked up at the white-headed man as one might look at a skyscraper. I don't think he would have been surprised if there had been clouds around Dr. Thomas' collar.

"Let's take a look at this young man," Dr. Thomas said in a loud, eager voice. He reached down, lifted my brother up, and placed him on the examination table.

Jeremiah's lower lip began to quiver.

"Don't cry," Dr. Thomas said briskly. "Don't cry, because if you do, I'll cry too, and we wouldn't want that now, would we? No, sir. How would that look if someone walked by and saw me crying? They would probably think, What is that silly old man doing, standing there crying?

"Open up," he said, inserting a tongue depressor in Jeremiah's mouth. "Aha, just as I thought—a high palate."

"Is that bad?" my mother asked nervously.

"Sixth one I've seen today. Probably seen over two hundred this year," he replied, raising his eyebrows.

"But what does that mean?" Dad asked.

"Means he probably had a lack of oxygen at some time," Dr. Thomas answered.

"Let's listen to your heart," he said, raising Jeremiah's shirt.

Jeremiah's lip started to quiver again.

"Shhh," Dr. Thomas shushed. "You don't want those other kids out there to think I'm pinching you or something, do you? If you start crying, then they'll all want to cry. Can you imagine how noisy it would be if all thirty-two kids were crying? Now that would really be a racket, wouldn't it? Nothing wrong with your heart, young man. No, sir. That ticker should last you a hundred years or more.

"Jeremiah, you've been a good boy," he said, with a quick smile. "Now, let's check your reflexes."

He tapped Jeremiah's knee and Jeremiah's leg jerked.

"Hey!" Dr. Thomas exclaimed. "How about that? Did you see your leg fly up? Let's do that again. There it goes! Now the other leg. Let's see if it will do the same thing. Yessir! Look at it go!"

At last Jeremiah laughed.

"Well, now, that's what I thought when you came in here," Dr. Thomas remarked. "I said to myself, I bet that Jeremiah Rodgers and I are going to be friends in no time. And sure enough, that's what we are."

"Look at what I have," Dr. Thomas said, raising his white eyebrows. "This is a pretty fancy light. Now, Jeremiah, you look at the light and I can take a good look at your eyes."

"Ah, just as I thought. They're *brown*. Whoops, no they aren't—they're blue. Thought you could fool me, didn't you? Well, you didn't."

(It became obvious that Dr. Thomas was keeping Jeremiah busy listening to his comments, while he quickly did the examinations. Pretty sneaky.)

While looking at Jeremiah's left eye, Dr. Thomas asked, "Mrs. Rodgers, has this eye always wandered toward the outside?"

"Yes," she answered. "We were told that it is because his eye muscles are weak."

"I don't think so," Dr. Thomas said abruptly. "I don't mean that I don't believe you were told that, but I don't believe that is true."

"We were told that it could be corrected by surgery. He could have had the operation before we came, but I thought we should wait."

"As far as I'm concerned it can wait forever," Dr. Thomas replied.

"What do you mean?"

"I mean, there's nothing wrong with his eye muscles. He has a vision problem, not a muscle problem."

"Do you mean he's blind in that eye?" Mom asked.

"Not far from it."

"Oh no," she gasped.

Dr. Thomas turned toward her. "Now don't get upset about that. Most of the kids we see here have vision problems. There's nothing wrong with having a vision problem. Some of my best friends have them. But I don't want Jeremiah to keep his. So I guess we'd better find a way to fix him up."

"Can you do that?" Mother wanted to know.

"I wouldn't be surprised," Dr. Thomas said with a smile edging across his face. "I wouldn't be surprised. But we're not going to let anybody cut on his muscles. No sir, not on this boy. I see a lot of kids come in here after such surgery. Most of those operations are useless. Turns my stomach."

He looked up. "If you go home and tell that other doctor I said that, he'll tell you I'm wrong and that I had no business telling you such a thing. But there are two reasons why I *should* tell you. One, because I'm old and I don't sugarcoat what I say. And two, because I'm right and he's wrong. Now I don't like being old, but I sure like being right! I don't want anybody operating on this kid's eyes, do you hear?"

"Yessir," my parents said.

Dr. Thomas patted Jeremiah on his back and turned toward us. "This is a great kid," he said. "I suspect that you're pretty good parents too. That's all for now."

Head Sizes and Chest Measurements

The measurement room turned out to be exactly as it sounded. Inside, two staff members, Elaine Lee and Hazel Doman, measured Jeremiah. They measured not only his height and weight but with special instruments they measured the circumference of his head. Then they very carefully recorded his chest measurement. As ticklish as Jeremiah was, getting those measurements was not an easy task. I thought it was going to take all of us to hold him still.

When they finally finished getting his chest statistics, Mother was concerned that he had squirmed too much for the figures to be accurate.

"I'm sure we have it," Mrs. Doman said. "We have handled a lot of squirmers."

"And we have bruises to prove it," Ms. Lee quipped.

"Really?"

"Sure," Ms. Lee said. "Some of our kids are pretty big and some are even more ticklish than Jeremiah. Others are frightened because they think we are going to hurt them. Boy, can their elbows and knees make bruises!"

"Are these measurements really important?" Dad asked. "I mean, could Jeremiah be kept off a therapy program because some measurement is too large or too small?"

"No, Mr. Rodgers," Mrs. Doman replied. "Most of the children we see here have smaller chests and heads than average children. In fact, most of them are smaller all over."

"It's obvious why you are concerned with heads since brains are your prime interest," Dad remarked, "but why are you so interested in chest sizes?"

"Because we know that the brain uses about twenty-five percent of the oxygen in our bodies," Mrs. Doman explained, "and, of course, lung capacity and chest expansion help determine how much oxygen we take in. Since we're concerned about brains, we're very concerned about oxyger and about chest sizes."

"I see," my father said.

You Have to Creep Before You Walk

The Mobility Building at The Institutes was a kids' paradise. Each and every room held wonders to behold. There were gym mats on the floors to tumble on, overhead ladders to swing on, large wooden boxes to climb on, balls to kick, and beanbags to throw. It seemed there should be a sign that read "Kids Only—No Adults Allowed."

However, once we saw how the equipment was used and how important it was to the therapy programs of these hurt children, the ladders and the floor mats no longer looked like playthings. They appeared to be what they were—tools to make children better.

Art Sandler asked Jeremiah to crawl across the floor. After several minutes of coaxing and a couple of threats from Mother, Jeremiah began crawling.

"Come on, Jeremiah," Mr. Sandler said excitedly. "That's the boy. Come on, you can do it. Come on, don't stop now. Keep going. That's it."

Finally, when Jeremiah reached the wall, Mr. Sandler yelled out, "Wow! That's great!"

Mom, Dad, Josh, and I all applauded. You would have thought my little brother had just won an Olympic medal or something.

"Very good," Mr. Sandler told him as he wrote some more comments in the growing folder.

Next he asked Jeremiah to creep on his hands and knees across the floor, but Jeremiah decided to be difficult. He went into one of his non-hearing, non-seeing moods and just sat there with a "no one's home" look on his face.

"Jeremiah, do as you're told," Mother scolded. Before our eyes, Jeremiah had escaped into that never-never land of his very own.

It was Josh who came to the rescue.

"Hey, Jeremiah," he said loudly enough to jolt our brother out of his trance. "Come on, I'll race you across the floor."

Jeremiah laughed and liked the idea well enough to give Josh a run for his money. He got down on his hands and knees and started after Josh. How Josh moaned and groaned as he let Jeremiah catch up with him, pretending that Jeremiah was too fast, and letting him win.

Josh assisted Mr. Sandler again by helping to get Jeremiah to throw a beanbag and to demonstrate that he could kick a ball.

Oh, boy, I thought, *there will be no living with Josh for the rest of the day.* His head grew five sizes.

Art Sandler walked over to Jeremiah, bent down, and suddenly picked him up by his heels, saying, "How would you like to swing upside-down?"

Although I expected Jeremiah to give out a bloodcurdling scream, he began to laugh instead. He liked it.

After Mr. Sandler let Jeremiah down, he came over to my parents and sat down. "Let me tell you what kinds of things I was testing Jeremiah for and what I found.

"We believe that it is very important for a child to become either completely left-sided or completely right-sided. Let me explain. Each of us has two brains—a left brain and a right brain. Due to crossovers, the right brain is responsible for the movement in the left side of our bodies, and the left brain is responsible for our right side. For some reason, nature decided that it is better if one brain becomes the leader and the other becomes the follower.

"In most people, the left brain becomes the leader, and, therefore, most of us human beings are right-handed. When the left brain is the leader, we have found that it is important for the person not only to be right-handed but right-footed, right-eared, and right-eyed. It is like an electric system: it seems to work better if all the main circuits are connected to the same source."

"Mr. Sandler," I interrupted, "may I ask a question?"

"Sure."

"I'm left-handed." (This wasn't a question at all but he understood what I was getting at.)

"And you are left-eyed and probably left-eared and left-footed, which means your right brain is probably the leader."

"Would it be better if I were left-brained and right-handed?" I asked.

"Not necessarily," he replied. "In your development, for some reason, your system chose to be right-brained and left-handed. It really doesn't seem to matter which side you choose, as long as you choose one side *all the way.*

"However," he said, "Jeremiah's system doesn't appear to have made that choice. He appears to be right-eyed but he threw the beanbag with his left hand. Sometimes he kicked the ball with his right foot and sometimes with his left. When he crept on his hands and knees, he did not creep in a good cross-pattern. When a child creeps, his left leg should move forward as his right hand moves forward. In other words, Jeremiah does not creep in a coordinated way. That is why he does not walk or run in a coordinated manner."

"Does that mean that Jeremiah will never be able to walk or run well?" Mother asked.

"Oh my gosh, no," Mr. Sandler said. "It doesn't mean that at all. But it does mean that he will probably not be able to walk and run well unless we get him to crawl and to creep properly."

"Does that mean that he will be accepted on the program?" Dad asked.

"No, it doesn't, Mr. Rodgers. There are other things to consider."

"Such as?"

"Such as—do we feel that the program will help him," Mr. Sandler answered.

"And do you?" Dad asked.

"Before you leave tonight, Glenn Doman will answer that question," Mr. Sandler said.

"Congratulations"

When she told us it would be a long day, Gretchen Kerr had been right.

It was now eight o'clock in the evening, and we were still not finished. We had one more person to see—Glenn Doman, the director of The Institutes. This was the meeting we were most anxious about, because he was the one who would tell us whether or not Jeremiah was brain-injured and whether or not this type of therapy might help him.

Since we were told that Mr. Doman would not be ready to see us for at least an hour, we went into The Institutes' dining room for dinner. All of us were so tired and so nervous about what we might be told that we didn't eat very much, except Josh, of course; he's never too tired or too nervous to stuff his face.

The one hour wait became two hours.

Dad was afraid we had been forgotten, so he went in to remind Mr. Doman's secretary that we were still waiting.

"He hasn't forgotten you, Mr. Rodgers," she told him. He's still with another family."

We waited.

We knew a little about Mr. Doman because Mom and Dad had read his book *How to Teach Your Baby to Read.* From the book jacket we had learned that during World War II Glenn was awarded the Distinguished Service Cross, the Silver Star, the Bronze Star, the British Military Cross, and many other decorations for bravery. For his work with brain-injured children he has been awarded the Roberto Simonsen Award from Brazil and the Brazilian Gold Medal of Honor. Mom and Dad had read newspaper articles and magazine stories about Mr. Doman, a physical therapist considered to be the main force and initiator of these new programs of therapy for which The Institutes had gained so much attention.

As with most new things, many people questioned whether or not these methods really worked. We realized there was no guarantee that Jeremiah could be made well by them.

It was ten thirty that night when our name was called. When we started toward the office Mother took my hand. I don't think she realized how tightly she held me. Although she was frightened, she tried not to show it. At last we would be told.

Which would it be?

Was Jeremiah's brain deficient?

   or was it psychotic??

   or was it injured???

I am sure we were all praying the same prayer: "Please, God, please let it be injured."

Mr. Doman did not make us wait long to learn the answer.

"Come right in," he said in a warm and friendly manner as he met us at the door.

He reached out to shake my parents' hands and said, "Congratulations, Mr. and Mrs. Rodgers. You have a brain-injured child."

Seeing Josh and me he said, "Well, it looks like we have all the Rodgers here." He shook Josh's hand and mine. "That's a good idea because you have a decision to make and it's best if it is a family decision."

Mother sat down and placed Jeremiah on her lap.

"Mrs. Rodgers," Mr. Doman told her, "you feel free to let Jeremiah down any time you want to. There is nothing in this room he could break that hasn't been broken before. As you have probably guessed by now, this place is for kids, and we happen to like having them here.

"Let me begin by answering some questions which I know you must have. First off, we believe that Jeremiah has had an injury to the midbrain."

"How do you know this?" Dad asked.

"You mean, how do we know this without having opened Jeremiah's head and looked inside at his brain and said, 'Ah yes, that's the part that's injured.' Is that what you're asking?"

"Yes."

"That's what I thought," he said. "Most people have very strange ideas about the brain. For instance, many people believe because it is inside a head, completely surrounded by bone, it is very difficult to reach the brain, but that is not the case at all. There are five pathways into the brain," he said, holding up five fingers. "They are seeing, hearing, feeling, tasting, smelling. I could affect all of our brains if I reached in a drawer, pulled out a gun, and fired it. First of all, the sight of the gun would frighten some of us; the sound would startle us; the smell of the gunpowder would annoy us; and if the bullet hit one of us, pain would be felt. Of course, we could even taste the gun, but I don't think we would like it. What I am saying is that the surgeon's knife is not the only means by which we can reach the brain.

"At the same time," he continued, "an electroencephalogram (EEG) is not the only way to find out how well a person's brain is functioning. In fact, the EEG tells us very little when compared to those things we can readily observe about brain function. For instance, when we see a long-distance runner win a race, we don't believe that his legs all by themselves won the race. We know that is not the case. What instructs

105

his legs to move in perfect coordination with the rest of his body? His brain, of course. What we see is a beautifully developed body, the result of hours of training, and magnificent brain function. The same is true of an opera singer, a ballerina, an artist, a writer, or whatever. The skill we appreciate is not talent but brain function and muscle responses. Do you see that?"

"Yes," we answered.

"Do you really? I hope you do because so much depends on your understanding."

He paused for a moment. "Perhaps even Jeremiah's life depends on how well you understand that brain function can be affected by stimulating the senses and that brain function can be seen by observing a person's skills as a human being."

"We understand," Mother said.

"Good," he said quickly. Then he turned to Josh and me and asked, "How about you two? Do you understand?"

"Yes, sir," we answered.

"That doesn't surprise me a bit," he said, smiling. "Children seem to understand very quickly, not because what I have just told you is so simple, because it isn't. It's taken mankind a million years to realize these things.

"Now then, let me make two more things clear. One—today our staff has made a decision about Jeremiah. We have decided that he is brain-injured, and if you wish we will accept him on one of our programs of therapy. Two—it is your decision whether or not you want to place him on one of our programs."

"If we didn't want a program for Jeremiah we wouldn't be here," Dad said firmly.

"Yes," Mr. Doman replied, "that may well be true, but believe me, Mr. and Mrs. Rodgers, it is really a rough program. You have no idea how demanding it can be. You have to arrange your whole household around it. It's an everyday program—*every day*. If you miss one day we'll boot you off the program without blinking an eye."

"What if Jeremiah should be sick?" my mother asked.

"If he is sick enough to be in the hospital, then you wouldn't be expected to do the program. Otherwise we would expect you to do it every day."

"Why is this program so demanding?" Dad asked.

"Because of Jeremiah," Mr. Doman answered.

"What do you mean?"

"Because even when parents do this program with their kids every day just as we tell them to, still some of them don't get well. We don't know why. They just don't. But this we do know: The kids who do their program every day without fail have a better chance of getting well than those who are given half a program or a program that is just done whenever their parents feel like doing it.

"So," he said, "if you decide you want to place him on a program, then I'm sure that you would want us to give you a program which has the best chance for success, not one which will be the easiest for you to do or the one which will be the easiest for our staff to show you how to do. You see, the answer is simple: The program has to be designed to give Jeremiah the best possible chance to get well. That's what makes it rough—really rough.

"What is really amazing," he continued, "is that so many parents do it. Sometimes they have impossible schedules yet are able to do more than they are told. As you may have noticed, we are really sold on parents here. We think parents are the greatest people in the world, and we're right."

"Mr. Doman," Mother said quietly, "I know why parents do it. They do it because no matter how rough your program may be, it can't possibly be as difficult as watching your child, day by day, and seeing that he isn't able to do the things other children his age can do. I've looked out our living-room window and watched the children across the street as they run and play their games. I realize that Jeremiah is not like those children. Every day those children are growing and learning. Every day the differences between them and Jeremiah are wider. Every day his chances for catching up with them or ever being able to do the things they can do are getting less and less. Don't tell me what is rough. No program in the world can be as difficult for a mother as having to stand by and watch her child left out and behind."

For a moment I held my breath. I was afraid Mr. Doman might think she was being rude or something.

Instead he smiled in a gentle way and said, "Of course, you're right, Mrs. Rodgers. That's why parents are able to do such extraordinary things.

"Now, then," he got back to the business at hand, "if you do decide to come back tomorrow and the remaining days of this week, here's what you can expect. Tomorrow, Jeremiah will be examined even further by our medical and therapy staffs so we will have an even more complete picture of how much he is injured."

"Is there a chance that you may find he is more brain-injured than you think now and he will not be accepted on the program?" Mother asked.

"No," he answered, "we have already concluded that he is brain-injured and that he is the kind we treat. You understand that many of our kids are in much worse shape than Jeremiah when they begin the program. Some of them are as blind as bats, deaf as doorknobs, and some of them can't even move their little fingers. Gosh, Jeremiah looks great for a starter. But don't be fooled into thinking that it will be easier to make him well. I assure you it will not be. Some of those really hurt kids may make great progress while Jeremiah's might be slow, slow, slow. Don't ask me why this is true, because I don't know the answer. I just know that it is true.

"The next two days Jeremiah will be with the other children. They will be taken care of by the staff while you, Mr. and Mrs. Rodgers, will be in the auditorium. You will be given extensive information as members of our staff lecture for twelve hours each day. We will teach you everything we know about brain function and brain injury. I believe that you will be able to do the things we tell you for Jeremiah without knowing the reasons for doing them. However, I am convinced that you can do them better if you know the reasons. In those two days we will give you the reasons.

"By the way," he said, "these lectures are for parents only, but," he said, looking at Josh and me, "if you like, I will make arrangements for Josh and M.J. to attend."

"Yes," we urged.

"But I must warn you. You must be absolutely quiet and not interrupt in any way. If you do I'll boot you out," he warned in a friendly way, but we knew he meant it.

"We'll be quiet," we promised.

"Friday," he said, "we will give you your program for Jeremiah and we will show you how to do each step of the program."

He stopped.

"Any questions?"

"Yes," Mother replied. "Do you know when Jeremiah was injured?"

"No. We don't know," he answered. "We have some guesses, but they are strictly guesses. My guess is that he was injured either sometime before, during, or shortly after he was born— probably due to a lack of oxygen."

(I thought of Dr. Thomas's remark about the roof of Jeremiah's mouth being high.)

"When he was injured really isn't important to you, to me, or even to Jeremiah," he told us. "It's like having an automobile accident. It's not important whether a wreck happened at one minute till twelve, at twelve o'clock noon, or at one minute after twelve. What is important is that there has been a collision. What is really important to us is that Jeremiah has had an injury to his brain and it's our job to try to fix him. Don't you agree?"

We agreed.

We liked Mr. Doman. He had a way of looking straight at us when he talked. When we had something to say he listened intently. For the time that we were in his office he acted as if we were the only people in the world. As we left we noticed that he still had three more families to see. It was a long day for him, too.

Except for Jeremiah, we were all dizzy with excitement. Mother and Dad were laughing and talking about how eager they were to start the program. Josh and I kept interrupting with our ideas.

When we got to the motel, Mother put Jeremiah in bed. Although the rest of us got in our beds, we couldn't turn off our excited thoughts or our mouths. We talked for hours. As I remember Mom and Dad were still talking when I finally fell asleep.

We had come such a long way with such high hopes.

Harold and Jimmy

Although we were not at The Institutes as long the second day as we had been the first, it seemed longer to Josh and me. Perhaps it was because some of the newness had worn off, but probably it was because we grew tired of waiting.

To help pass the time we made bets about some of the children who had been brought there as patients. Of those we had seen the day before, we tried to decide which ones were brain-injured and which ones were not.

Thinking back, such calloused attitudes make me wonder about Josh and me. Anyway, thats how we spent most of our morning -- snooping around to see who "won" and who "lost."

I thought that extremely thin little boy who had to be lifted into and out of his wheelchair would

113

not be back. Glenn Doman had said that many of the children would be in worse condition than Jeremiah, but that kid really looked like he was in bad shape. He made strange groaning sounds when he tried to talk. And his hands and legs were terribly twisted and bent. And, well, he didn't look as if he had much upstairs—you know what I mean—in the intelligence department.

His name was Harold. He was twelve years old, but he looked more like a medium-sized nine or a very little ten.

Both Josh and I missed on Harold—he was back. As for the intelligence department, we struck out on that, too. It seems that Harold couldn't talk or move about very well, but he could read over a thousand words a minute and enjoyed college calculus books. In other words, the kid was a genius—a brain-injured genius to boot.

Before meeting Harold I had the idea that if someone was brain-injured, automatically he was not very bright. Not so. It depends on which part of the brain is injured. Harold was a perfect example. His arms and legs didn't work well, but his thinking was super.

Obviously I needed to throw out some of my old ideas to make room for these ~~new~~ new ones. Harold's being bright and brain-injured at the same time was something new to me and I had to think about that for a while.

To add to my confusion, there was Jimmy—thirteen years old (two years older than I was), who looked exactly like David Cassidy (only shorter), and an absolute vision!

I liked him the moment I saw him. Quite by chance we happened to be seated across from each other at lunch. Well, not exactly by chance, and not directly across from each other, but close enough that it would have been rude if we hadn't spoken. So we spoke. Before we knew it we were talking to each other about our schools, the cities we were from (he was from Denver), favorite sports (he liked to ski), and pets (he had a raccoon).

Well, we were getting along famously. I thought, *Gee, this is really great. I'll have someone to talk to this afternoon besides Josh.*

Then (me with my big mouth—when will I ever learn to keep it shut?), I told Jimmy that we were at The Institutes because my little brother was brain-injured. That wasn't the bad part. I had to open my mouth even wider and ask him if it was his brother or a sister who had problems.

"I don't have a brother or a sister," he answered.

I knew the answer to my next question when it was no more than halfway out of my mouth but I couldn't stop. The words just kept coming out like cans falling from a stack in a supermarket display.

"Then why are you here?" I asked in all stupidity.

"Because I'm brain-injured," he answered.

"You don't look brain-injured," I said, because I was too dumb to think of anything smarter to say.

"I have *dyslexia,*" he said.

"What?"

"Dyslexia."

"Really?"

"Yes."

I started to ask if it was "catching," but I finally stopped myself and asked, instead, "What's that?"

"It's a medical word," he answered.

"What does it mean?" I wanted to know.

"It means I can't read."

"You're kidding."

"Scout's honor," he said holding up his right hand.

"Can't you read anything?"

"Not much," he replied, "because I can't make out what the words are supposed to be."

"How awful," I exclaimed, then wanted to shake myself again. "I don't mean that *you're* awful; I mean, that must really be frustrating for you."

"It is," he said, "but I'm not as bad as Herbert Knickerson. He goes to the same school I do; he has *acute* dyslexia."

"What does that mean?"

"It's a medical term that means he *really* can't read."

"Is there a medical term for people who *can* read?" I asked.

"I don't know," he replied.

That's what I mean about new ideas and having

to readjust my thinking. There was Harold—he didn't look as if he were bright, but he was a genius. And then there was Jimmy, who was just a great looking kid, who looked and talked as if he was smart as a whip, and he couldn't read. Now, if that's not the best example of why you shouldn't judge a book by its cover, I'll eat my leather bookmark.

Later in the afternoon, when I saw Jimmy again, we got along even better. I really liked him, but I wasn't quite sure what I would tell my friends back home.

"Guess what! I met the neatest brain-injured boy at The Institutes! And he liked me, too." That would go over like a lead balloon.

"If I give you my address, will you write to me when you get home?" Jimmy asked.

"What good would that do, if you can't read it?" my mouth replied without waiting for my head to think.

"M.J.," Jimmy said slowly and clearly, so I might understand both his words and their meaning, "I hope that I will be better soon. That's why I'm here, you know."

If I told myself once, I told me a thousand times that afternoon, "M.J., you've got a dumb mouth. That's what's wrong with you. You're dumb. That's what you are. You're dumb, dumb, dumb."

How awful!

Winter in July

The third morning, as we had been told, we took Jeremiah to the clinic building. When he realized that we were going to leave him with the other children and the staff members, his lower lip quivered and his large blue eyes watered a little. But he didn't cry as we thought he would.

We made sure that we were in the auditorium before nine o'clock; we had been warned that if we were one minute late we would not be admitted.

I wondered if those who were late would really be turned away. By nine o'clock all the chairs in the auditorium were filled. I noticed that there were exactly the same number of chairs as there were people. And at exactly nine o'clock, the door opened and Glenn Doman walked into the room.

Mother had told us that morning to wear our coats because she had heard that the auditorium would be cold. It was. When I asked Mother why the room was so cold, she said she wasn't sure but there was probably a reason for it. We soon learned the reason.

"Good morning," Mr. Doman said with a friendly smile. "This could be the most important day of your lives. I want you to listen to me as you've never listened before."

I thought he looked straight at me as I reached up to button the collar of my coat.

"You may have noticed that this room is cold. It's cold on purpose," he said. "It's cold for you. It is cold for your kids. If this room were made warm and comfortable, you would have a hard time listening and paying attention. Some of you would even fall asleep."

His voice grew louder. "You can't afford to go to sleep today. Your child can't afford for you to sleep. I would rather that all of us ended up with colds than to take the chance that you might miss one important piece of information which could mean the difference between your child's getting well or not getting well.

"In these next two days members of our staff are going to tell you what we have spent all of our lives finding out. We will tell you all we know about brain-injured children. These hours are carefully planned and we will get everything into these two days if we keep on schedule and stay with the subject. Let me tell you the rules:

"First rule," he said raising his index finger. "No interruptions. We'll stop every so often and ask for questions. When we do, ask only about things we have said up to that time. Don't ask us about things we will discuss later because if you do we'll waste a lot of time. I promise you that before you finish here tomorrow night, you will have a chance to ask any question you may have.

"We will answer your questions in one of three ways: give you an answer, tell you we'll answer later, or tell you that we don't know the answer."

As Glenn Doman spoke, I glanced back at the clock. It was fifteen minutes after nine. The first fifteen minutes had passed quickly, but what would twelve hours be like? I tried to imagine. It would be like sitting through *Gone with the Wind* three and one-half times. No, not quite the same because that would be watching two and a half repeats. It would be more like seeing *Gone with the Wind, Ben Hur, Dr. Zhivago,* and *Mary Poppins* all on the same day. I looked over at Josh and knew exactly what he was thinking—two doubleheaders. He breathed a long sigh and leaned back in his chair.

I looked around the room to see if the parents, too, were thinking about the hours which lay ahead of them. They didn't show it. They all appeared to be extremely interested in what Mr. Doman was saying.

Then I noticed the headsets. Some of the parents were wearing earphones. I wondered why; then I realized that the French parents were wearing them. So were the Italians, the Spaniards, and Japanese. I looked toward the back of the auditorium and saw a large window. I could see the translators in glass booths relaying what Mr. Doman was saying in these other languages—like a meeting of the United Nations.

Suddenly, I thought of Jeremiah and the other children who were waiting for their parents. In a way they were waiting for what the parents would learn in this room. Then I understood what Mr. Doman had meant. This could be the most important day in these children's lives. Shivers ran up my spine—not because I was cold but because I realized what an important time it was.

I reached down and picked up the notebook I had brought with me. Quietly, I opened the cover, placed it on the desk before me, and began to make notes.

I might mention that during the following school year, these notes were used as a basis for a science report for which I received an "A-." The "A" was for the quality of the written matter, and the minus was for my drawings, which I thought was terribly unfair. After class, I told Mr. Richards that since his was a science class and not an art course, I felt I should not be graded down because of my inability to draw. He told me that he was sorry I felt that way, but he didn't offer to change the grade. I hope someday Mr. Richards reads this book and realizes that now the whole world knows what a crumb he was. Of course since my pictures are in the book too it is possible some of the readers will agree with Mr. Richards' decision.

Anyway, the following paragraphs are taken from that report. A word of warning to the reader: I hope you don't get the idea that these paragraphs contain dull, scientific information and skip over them in order to get on with the story. In the first place, if you have a brain you will find the information fascinating, because you'll learn some things about the mysterious marvel you have inside your head. Second, this information *is* an important part of Jeremiah's story. If you are going to really understand what was the matter with my brother, why the world appeared strange to him, why he appeared strange to the rest of the world, then you simply must know some of these important things about the brain.

That Marvel of Marvels--The Human Brain

By M.J. Rodgers

The brain is the information center for our bodies. It receives messages through our five senses: seeing, hearing, tasting, smelling, feeling; yet it lives in silence and darkness; without feeling and without sensation. It is the analyzer of the information which is supplied by the senses. When all of its parts are functioning and all of its circuits are intact, we are able to do those things which are expected of human beings.

So important is the brain, that it is
protected more than any other organ in our
body. It is shielded by bone and is en-
closed in a fluid to cushion it from hits
on the head.

The brain is composed of over one
hundred billion brain cells.

To try to give some meaning to this
number, if one were born before Jesus of
Nazareth and used a brand-new brain cell
every ten seconds, sixty seconds a minute,
sixty minutes an hour, twenty-four hours
a day, three hundred and sixty-five days a
year, until today, there would still be
more than three billion neurons (brain cells)
left to use.

It is estimated that we use only ten
percent of these billions of cells. Although
the brain makes up only 2 percent of our
body's weight, it uses 20 percent of the
oxygen we take in. The brain never sleeps
although its owner must rest. It can receive and analyze hundreds of pieces of
information at the same time. It can tell
the difference between reality, memory, and
fantasy.

"The human brain," says Glenn Doman,
"is a superb computer, and it is far better
organized than are its mechanical copies.
The more that's put into the human brain
the more it will hold; the more it is used

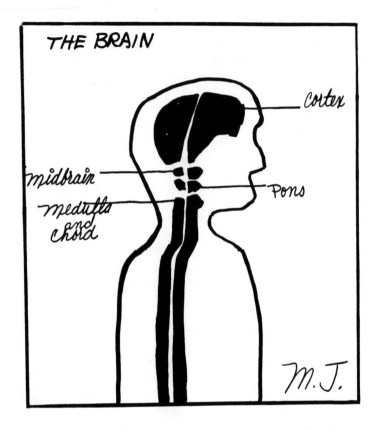

the better it works. The function of the
brain is to relate its owner to his environ-
ment."

Due to the function of the human brain,
people are able to do things that no other
animals can do.

Only human beings can stand up and
walk in a cross pattern.

Only human beings can talk in an abstract, symbolic language. (That means they can discuss ideas.)

Only human beings can see in such a way that they can read that language.

Only human beings can hear in such a way that they can understand that language when they hear it.

Only human beings can oppose their thumbs to their forefingers and are able to write that language.

Only human beings can feel an object and know what it is without seeing it, tasting it, smelling it, or hearing it.

To my surprise the morning in the auditorium passed quickly. We were told we would have one hour for lunch and that we must be back in our seats, ready to begin the afternoon session, at one o'clock.

At the time, we couldn't help but wonder what Jeremiah thought about being left with the other children. In my mind, I pictured him sitting alone in a corner of one of the rooms with tears streaming down his cheeks. These illusions quickly faded when we looked in the window and saw him laughing. He was throwing a ball to one of the staff members. We were relieved.

There surely were moments, however, when he wondered where we had gone and why we had left him with strangers.

Brain Programs

At one o'clock we were in the auditorium again. It was not warmer. If anything it was colder. And everyone was wide awake.

"We have found," Glenn Doman said, "that brain-injured children, no matter what their ages, cannot do one or all of four things properly: move their arms and legs, crawl, creep, or walk. All of these things we expect in the development of a one-year-old child, but a brain-injured child cannot do at least one of them. Some cannot do two; some cannot do three; and there are some who cannot do any of the four.

"Each of these four mobility functions—moving arms and legs, crawling, creeping, and walking—is controlled by the brain. We believe that each in return is important to the development of the brain.

"It is terribly important that you understand this," he stressed.

"We have found that when children who cannot move their arms and legs properly are shown how to move their arms and legs properly, they get better.

"When children who cannot crawl properly are programmed to crawl properly, they get better.

"When children who cannot creep or walk properly are programmed to do these things properly, they get better.

"In other words, we can affect the functions of brains and we can improve the quality of their functions."

He paused for a moment and looked at us thoughtfully.

"I told you this morning that each of us has over ten billion brain cells and that we use only about one tenth of them. Nine-tenths we never use, but they are there. If all the brain cells in a child's head were dead, the child would be dead. What if only a part of that 10 percent that he uses is injured, but the other nine tenths is okay—just not being used? If we had a way, or ways, to make the child start using those other cells, then there's a good chance he could do all the things other kids his age can do.

"The brain is like a computer. It has to be programmed. For instance, no kid is born in the United States speaking and understanding English. No baby born in Spain understands Spanish or in France who understands French.

We program English into them in the United States. If we were French, we would program French into them.

"If a child is brain-injured, his programs often have to be more intense, repeated with more frequency, or performed for longer periods of time in order to strengthen the pathways to his brain.

"We will show you how to program the brains of your children with frequency, intensity, and duration. As you will see, we have some clever ways to do that.

"For those children who have mobility problems we will give you a mobility program. Those who have hearing problems will have an auditory program; speech problems—a speech program; seeing problems—a vision program; and reading problems—a reading program."

One mother spoke out. "My child doesn't have just one of those problems. Mark has all of those problems."

"Yes, I know," Mr. Doman replied. "I doubt that there is one kid here this week who has only one problem. Some may have only a couple of problems—can't creep properly and can't read well.

"Others may have three or four problems, and there are some here who have so many problems that if we stayed up all night we couldn't count all of them. For instance, there is one boy who can't read, write, walk, talk, turn over, feed himself, or hear. He can't go to the store by himself. He can't sit up. He can't use a telephone. He can't tell anyone that he doesn't feel well or where it hurts, and on and on. In fact, this kid can't even breathe well. He is a human being who can't do most of the things that human beings are supposed to be able to do. In fact there are newborn babies who can do things this twelve-year-old boy cannot do."

Another mother spoke up. "My daughter has a speech problem, a mobility problem, and a hearing problem. Which program would we begin?"

Doman smiled. "Probably all three," he said. "Let me explain. In truth, your daughter has only *one* problem and that problem is called brain injury. Because she is brain-injured, she is not physically as coordinated as she should be; she does not hear as well as she should and she does not speak as well as other children her age. The cause of her problems is in the brain—not in her ears, mouth, arms, legs, or little finger. The trouble is in her brain.

"What our staff will do is to give you programs of therapy for you to do with your children. The purpose of these programs is to place good information into your children's brains.

"You see, the children who do not move properly do not move properly because they do not know how it feels to move properly.

"The children who do not speak well do not speak well because they don't know how it feels to speak well.

129

"The children who do not see well do not see well because they don't know how it feels to see well.

"Your child's therapy program will be designed to show your child's brain how it feels to move, to hear, and to speak like a human being.

"As you will see on Friday when the staff members give you the programs and show you how to do them, you will probably be given several programs. To do one of these may take only a few minutes a day. But every program you will be given will have to be done every day. The more programs you have, the more time it will take to do them.

"I promise you this," he said. "We will give you every shortcut we know, but we will never shortcut your kid's chances by shortening *your* time or *our* time. These programs are set up to give your kid the best chance of getting well. They are not set up to give parents plenty of rest or our staff members coffee breaks."

He looked down at the floor for a moment, then back up at the audience. "There are people who say that these programs are impossible and that we expect too much for the parents.

"That is probably true," he said.

"There are people who say it would be impossible to do these programs in schools and clinics because they require so much individual attention.

"I think that is true.

130

"Some say that the only reason parents begin these programs is that they are so desperate to make their children well that they will try anything.

"I think that is true.

"I am convinced that you are the only people on the face of this earth who love your children so fiercely, and who believe so intently that it is worth whatever time it takes to make your child well, that you will try the impossible. I think parents are the only people who can muster that kind of determination.

"There are people who say that all children who are placed on these programs do not get completely well.

"This is true.

"However, many of them do get well. The interesting thing is that most of these children's parents were told that their conditions were hopeless. As I look about the room, it occurs to me that most of you have been told the same thing. *You* don't believe they are. That's why you are here. *We* don't believe they are either or we wouldn't be giving you programs of therapy.

"Chances are," he told us, "some of your children will not get completely well, but we don't know which ones; some will get well, but we don't know which ones. I can't promise that all children who are well today will be well tomorrow. I can only promise you a lot of work, tired muscles, and long days. If you do the things we tell you, if our staff keeps working to find even better methods, if we have a lot of luck, and if the good Lord smiles on us, maybe—just maybe—your kid will be a winner. As long as we have hope that this can be, then no one can say that your child is hopeless."

The day had grown into night, yet for several more hours the parents asked questions. Finally all the questions were answered. We were bone-tired and we were cold, but we were still wide awake.

During the course of the two days we spent in the auditorium, many members of the medical, educational, and therapy staffs spoke to us. Dr. Roselise Wilkerson spoke to us about nutrition. Dr. Robert Dr. Robert Doman spoke on the causes of brain injury. Dr. Edwinn LeWinn told us of recent medical findings which support the work of the Institutes. Dr. Evan Thomas gave us a look at history and the brain-injured child. Gretchen Kerr told of the stages of development of average children and how brain-injured children can be compared to normal children. Art Sandler compared the development and function of children with the evolution of man. My dad said that these two days were organized organized better than most college courses.

As you can see, if I told everything about

those two days, this book would be longer
than _War and Peace_.

 Since Glenn Doman is the man responsible
for most of the ideas and is director of the
Institutes, and to save a ~~great~~ great deal of time
I have told only about the sessions with him.

M. J.

Pandora's Folder

When the alarm rang on Friday morning, I wouldn't have been surprised if one of us had reached over and strangled the clock.

Oooooooh! We were tired. Our bodies groaned with pain; our eyes felt as though they had been sandpapered, and our heads felt like they were stuffed with metal bricks.

"Don't anyone say a word until I have had at least six cups of coffee," Dad said.

"Please," Mother groaned, "someone point me toward the closet."

"Do I have to brush my teeth?" Josh wanted to know.

"Not if you don't want breakfast," Mother told him.

"Oh, okay," he moaned.

Josh would have brushed a picket fence for food. All of us moved about the room like zombies—except Jeremiah. He wasn't tired at all.

He ran around the room making noises like a dive bomber. We kept hoping he would either run out of fuel or lose his voice.

Breakfast was as solemm as a funeral. No one looked up from his plate. Out of the corners of our eyes we could see that Jeremiah was making a mess with his cereal. We ignored him. Boy, did the waitress give us a dirty look when we got up to leave. Dad handed her a dollar, shrugged his shoulders, and said, "Sorry, honey."

By nine o'clock we were back at The Institutes, and we were beginning to look and talk like people once again.

"Good morning," Art Sandler said as we entered the room.

"Good morning," we replied with forced cheerfulness.

In the center of the room stood a sturdy table with a padded plastic top.

"This," Mr. Sandler said, patting the table with his hand, "is a patterning table. As you can see it is built for use, not for beauty. The one you will build for Jeremiah should be twenty-four inches wide and at least one foot longer than he is. We will give you printed instructions before you leave.

"Mr. Rodgers, will you put Jeremiah up on the table, please?" he asked.

"Sure. Come on, boy," Dad said, lifting Jeremiah up and setting him on the table.

Jeremiah's lower lip began to quiver and tears started to fill his eyes.

"There, there now," Mr. Sandler said to him. "This isn't going to hurt in any way. All we're going to do is move your arms and legs."

Hearing that, Jeremiah's mouth opened and the loudest squawl I have ever heard bellowed out. One would have thought someone had just threatened to cut his head off.

We tried to quiet him, but the more we talked to him the louder he cried.

"Maybe we'd better wait," Mother suggested.

"No," Mr. Sandler said, over Jeremiah's screams. "We might just as well do it now. Let's turn him over on his stomach."

Dad turned Jeremiah over and Mother helped to hold him down.

Mr. Sandler placed his hand on each side of Jeremiah's head. "This is the way to hold his head," he said. "Notice that my thumbs curve around his ears, never allowing my hands to cover them completely."

He raised Jeremiah's head slightly and turned it to the right, letting it rest on his left hand.

"You lift his head just high enough to allow the chin to pass over the tabletop without rubbing it," Mr. Sandler instructed us.

As he began to turn my brother's head from side to side in an even rhythm, Jeremiah cried even louder.

"The rhythm is very important," Mr. Sandler said. "The speed is not as important as that a definite rhythm be established. And it is the person at the head who establishes the rhythm."

"Can we go too fast?" Dad called out over Jeremiah's howls.

"Yes," Mr. Sandler called back. "If you go too fast, he might get dizzy and your patterners will tire before the five minutes are over."

"Now you try it," he said to Mother.

Mother walked over and carefully placed her hands on his head and started to turn it. "Don't cry," she said, trying to calm him.

Then Dad tried it.

"You, too," Mr. Sandler said to me. "You'll probably be doing this, too, when you get home."

"Do you think she can?" Mother asked (which didn't shoot my confidence up to the ceiling).

"Of course she can," Mr. Sandler said firmly. "We've found that kids are often better patterners than adults."

I took hold of Jeremiah's head and began to turn it back and forth.

Then Josh took a turn.

Mr. Sandler showed us how to move Jeremiah's arms and legs.

"The right hand is placed in front of his face while the left leg is straight. As his head is turned to the left, the right hand is moved straight down the table, as if you were painting the tabletop with it. Then the hand is raised slightly and brought to rest on his bottom. At the same time, slide his right leg forward to a right angle bend."

Jeremiah did not like the arm and leg movements any better than he liked his head being turned.

However, within a few minutes we seemed to understand what we were to do. Mother was turning Jeremiah's head; Dad was moving his right arm and leg, while I was moving his left arm and leg.

We were patterning.

"You are programming his brain," Mr. Sandler said. "You are showing it how it feels to crawl in a coordinated way."

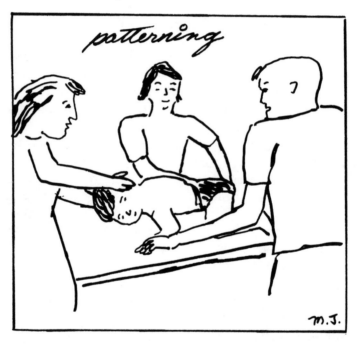

As we patterned him, Jeremiah finally stopped crying. I don't think he decided that he liked the patterning, but he probably finally realized that we were bigger than he was and we were going to pattern him whether he liked it or not.

"You are to pattern Jeremiah four times a day for five minutes at a time," Mr. Sandler told us. "You are to do this every day—Monday, Tuesday, Thanksgiving, Christmas—every day.

"As soon as you finish each patterning, immediately place Jeremiah on the floor and have him crawl on his stomach for five minutes."

"But he can walk," my mother said.

"But he doesn't walk well, does he?"

"No, but..."

"The reason he does not walk well is that he never crawled well," Mr. Sandler reminded us. "If you want him to walk well, then he must crawl."

"But how do we get him to do it if he doesn't want to?" she asked.

Mr. Sandler looked at her for a moment. "The same way you get him to do anything else. First you say, 'Jeremiah, will you please get down and crawl?' If he does, fine. If he doesn't, you say, 'Jeremiah, get down on the floor and crawl or I'll pop you one.' If he does, fine. If he doesn't—pop!"

"But couldn't that cause emotional problems?" Dad asked.

"You'll get over them," he said.

"I mean, couldn't it cause emotional problems for Jeremiah?" Dad said.

Mr. Sandler looked at Dad and replied. "Mr. Rodgers, we're talking about making Jeremiah *well*, not about his likes and dislikes. If he had a fever and the doctor told you to give him a

139

medicine, would you first ask Jeremiah if he liked the medicine? Of course you wouldn't. You'd say, 'Here, kid, take this.' You wouldn't fool around about it. It's the very same with this program. If he likes it, fine. If he doesn't, it's up to you to see that it is done anyway."

"I understand," Mother replied tightening her lips. "Jeremiah," she said, firmly, "come on, it's time to crawl."

Dad was right. He didn't like it.

Mr. Sandler was also right. Jeremiah was going to crawl whether he liked it or not.

After fifteen minutes of Jeremiah's crying and saying "no" at the top of his lungs, and with all of us trying to get him to crawl across the floor, we finally got him to move for a couple of minutes.

After we had given a sigh of relief, Mr. Sandler then told us that Jeremiah would also have to creep on his hands and knees for five minutes after each crawling session.

Jeremiah didn't like to creep any better than he liked to crawl, but he finally did it.

creeping

Then we followed Mr. Sandler into another room. Once inside, we saw an overhead ladder. Its height could be adjusted.

"You'll also be given instructions for building one of these," Mr. Sandler told my father. "We want to increase Jeremiah's chest size as quickly as possible. We want him to *brachiate* across this ladder for one minute at a time, eighteen times a day."

"Do what?" Dad asked.

"Brachiate," Mr. Sandler explained. "Hang by his hands and swing from one rung to another."

141

"Like this," Josh said, jumping up and grabbing hold of one of the rungs and reaching out for the next one. "Like a monkey." Josh laughed.

"That's right," Mr. Sandler agreed.

"But Jeremiah's hands aren't very strong," my mother said. "I don't think he can do that."

"That's just the point," Mr. Sandler replied. "If he doesn't do things which challenge him physically, his hands won't get stronger. Mrs. Rodgers, very few children who start the

brachiating

m.J.

programs can do these things in the beginning. What you must do is to get him to do them as soon as possible."

Mr. Sandler lifted Jeremiah up and told him to take hold of one of the rungs. As he was told, he took hold with both hands and Mr. Sandler slowly let go of him. When Jeremiah realized he was hanging by himself, his lower lip started again, but before the tears began to flow, Mr. Sandler said, "Hey, everyone. Look at Jeremiah. He's doing it all by himself!"

We applauded and Jeremiah, with a smile of pride, forgot about crying and instead began to laugh.

"Like a monkey," he said.

Then we laughed, too.

For a few minutes at least, Jeremiah seemed to be enjoying himself.

"One more trick," Art Sandler said. He bent down and picked Jeremiah up by his ankles, letting him hang upside-down. When Mr. Sandler started swinging him back and forth, Jeremiah really laughed. When he finally let him down, Jeremiah kept asking for more. He got several more swings. When it looked as if it was going to become an all-day swinging session, he was finally put down and told, "No more."

Then Mr. Sandler showed us a foot strap that we could put on Jeremiah to hang him by his heels from the ladder and swing him back and forth.

"As you can see," Mr. Sandler said, "He's going to like this. That's good, because it is very good for him. Turning him upside-down allows gravity to increase the blood supply to his head. Better blood supply means more oxygen for the brain, and that's what we're after. Do this only one minute at a time, eighteen times a day."

Mr. Sandler handed my mother a manila folder, and she wrote down all the things we had been told to do.

"Is that all?" Mother asked when Mr. Sandler finished.

"That's it," he said.

"Well," Mother said with a sigh, "that's not as bad as I thought it might be."

"Oh, that's not *all*," Mr. Sandler replied. "I meant that's all *I'm* going to give you to do. The other staff members will tell you what else you are going to do."

"You mean there really is more?" Mother asked.

"Yes, I'm sure there is," he said.

Mother looked down at the folder.

"More!" Jeremiah suddenly yelled out. "More!"

"Oh, be quiet," Mother said, not knowing whether to laugh or cry.

"I don't know if we can do it," she said quietly.

My father said nothing.

"I know it looks impossible," Mr. Sandler told us. "But it isn't. Hundreds of parents are doing it."

"Maybe they're braver or stronger than we are," she replied.

"Maybe they are," Mr. Sandler said. "But I don't think so. I think the Rodgers will do just fine."

"I hope so," Mother said closing the folder. "Who do we see now?"

He told us to go back to the activity room and we would be told.

Within the next four hours that manila folder was opened and closed many times. Each time it

145

was opened, another piece of information went inside and some additional therapy was added to Jeremiah's program. Because it was stuffed with more instructions than it appeared it could possibly hold, Mother called it Pandora's folder.

By late afternoon Jeremiah's daily program of therapy looked as follows:

Pattern—five minutes—four times
After patterning—crawl—five minutes
After crawling—creep five minutes
Eye exercise—five minutes—four times

We were to do each of the following with him eighteen times:

Hang upside-down—one minute
Brachiate—one minute
Roll and somersault—one minute
Crawl—two minutes
Creep—two minutes

We were to teach him to read words which were familiar to him such as *Mom, Dad, hand, foot, door, dog,* and so on. We were to print the words in red on large cards so they would be easier for him to see.

We were told that we should talk to him and tell him names of things even if he did not ask.

We were to get a variety of small objects that he was to feel with his hands and tell us what they were without seeing them.

However, some things we were told not to do

for him. We were supposed to give him the opportunity to feed himself (no matter what a mess he made) and the chance to dress and undress himself (even if it took a long, long time).

Finally we were told which foods and vitamins were best for him.

When we got into the car that evening and started back for the hotel, I thought everyone would be excited about the program and would want to talk about it again until late into the night.

Instead, the "blahs" we had felt that morning returned.

Dad said, "I think I could sleep for a year."

Mother said, "I think I'm going to have a headache."

Josh said, "I wish we were home."

Jeremiah just turned over and went to sleep.

I got the point; no one wanted to talk about anything. We rode along in the car, pretending the others weren't there.

I looked at the houses we passed. The lights in the windows looked so peaceful and lovely. I wondered if the people in those houses were happy or if they had troubles of their own. I had no way of knowing about their lives and they had no way of knowing that my little brother was brain-injured and needed so much help.

It suddenly struck me as being very sad.

The Long Talk Home

The two days it took us to drive from Philadelphia to Indianapolis turned out to be one long discussion. Mother and Dad went over and over the things we had heard and seen.

"Do you really believe it's possible to activate brain cells?" Mother asked.

And Dad answered, "I'm not sure."

"Then you don't really believe it," she said.

"That wasn't what I said."

"But that's what you meant."

"That's not what I meant. I meant what I said. I don't know."

"Then how can we do the program if you don't know and if I'm not sure?" she asked.

"You don't have to believe in falling in order to fall," Dad stated matter-of-factly.

"Falling has nothing to do with it," Mother retorted.

148

"Of course it does," Dad replied. "You don't have to believe in something for it to work. It's just like falling: If you stub your toe, you may fall whether you believe in gravity or not; its force works for both believers and nonbelievers."

"It's not the same," she said, gritting her teeth. "I strongly feel that the program would work better if all of us believed in it."

"If we don't do the program, what will we do?" Dad asked.

"I don't know anything else to do. So we'll do it, of course," she answered. "But I only wish we were surer of it. What if it works for all the other children who were there last week, but not for Jeremiah?"

"Then we fail," Dad said.

"I don't see how you can sit there and say such a thing," she snapped back. "That's really the most brutal thing I've ever heard you say!"

"But it's true," he replied. "Either we succeed or we fail. It's as simple as that."

"If you say that once more, I'm going to be angry," Mother warned.

"Okay," he said, bringing a halt to the conversation.

After a while Mother spoke again. "I just wish we were completely convinced. However, I suppose we don't have to be convinced for it to work."

"Exactly," Dad said. "It's like falling."

Mother's voice revealed her anger. "If you

mention *falling* to me one more time, I'm going to scream!"

During the next one hundred miles, not another word was spoken.

Finally, someone would say something like, "Oh, look at that beautiful tree," or "Look, there's a lake," or "When are we going to stop to eat?" (The last was Josh). Then we all started talking again, but within a matter of minutes, Mom and Dad were in another argument. Josh and I would try to stay out of the way—which is a neat trick when you're packed like sardines in a car.

Have you ever noticed that when children get into an ~~arus~~ argument adults can't wait to jump in and tell them to cut it out? But if adults get into a disagreement, they don't want any interruptions--especially from children. That's another thing. When kids argue, adults tell them that they are acting like children, when they could just as easily say, "You're acting like adults." It's a thought worth thinking about, but not one to mention to adults--especially when their tempers are heated.

I have heard some people say that adults should never argue in front of children. I don't know about that. If we don't hear them do it, how are we supposed to know that it's *all right* to scream at each other when we're grown up?

Perhaps I should not have mentioned that my parents argued, but I don't see why not, because they did. Sometimes their arguments seemed silly. Sometimes they were loud; sometimes they were terribly frightening; and sometimes they were frustrating. Most of the ones they had about Jeremiah's problems were the frustrating kinds, because they came from fear. They were afraid that he wouldn't get well or that they would not do the right things for him. They were afraid that even if they did all the right things, he would not be changed enough to grow up, and have a job, and be able to have a family of his own. They were afraid of all these things. I understood it. And although he never said, I think Josh understood it too.

151

All Present and Accounted For

When we arrived home our real test as a family began. You probably won't believe this. If I read it in a book I wouldn't believe it either—even if there were signed documents and pictures, I wouldn't believe. After we had spent two whole days together in the car, the day after we got home Dad called a family meeting. "A review and planning meeting" he titled it. It wouldn't surprise me if someday Dad becomes the president of something.

"The meeting is called to order."

Although Dad did not stand up, it was obvious that he was going to make a speech—a long one. My only defense against long speeches is to get a terribly interested expression on my face and think about something else, such as what am I going to do for this year's science project, or should I try out for the school play.

In between my inner thoughts I opened up for outer signals so I could at least keep up with the drift of Dad's commentary.

He covered the early years of Jeremiah's life, the hopes and fears, the wait-and-sees, and all those grim things we had lived through. Then he recapped what we had been told at The Institutes and had Mother show us a schedule she had typed out.

When I saw the schedule, I woke up. It appeared as follows:

DAILY SCHEDULE

7:15	Sequence 1	
	Crawl	2 minutes
	Creep	2 minutes
	Roll and somersault	1 minute
	Brachiate	1 minute
	Hang upside down	1 minute
7:30	Breakfast	1 hour

(because Jeremiah eats so slowly)

8:30	Sequence 2	
	Crawl	2 minutes
	Creep	2 minutes
	Roll and somersault	1 minute
	Brachiate	1 minute
	Hang upside down	1 minute

153

8:45	Sequence 3	
	Crawl	2 minutes
	Creep	2 minutes
	Roll and somersault	1 minute
	Brachiate	1 minute
	Hang upside down	1 minute

9:00	First patterning	5 minutes
	Crawl	5 minutes
	Creep	5 minutes
	Brachiate	1 minute
	Hang upside down	1 minute
	Roll and somersault	1 minute
	Eye Exercises	5 minutes

9:30	Second patterning	5 minutes
	Crawl	5 minutes
	Creep	5 minutes
	Brachiate	1 minute
	Hang upside down	1 minute
	Roll and somersault	1 minute
	Eye exercise	5 minutes

| 10:00 | Reading program | 10 minutes |

| 10:20 | Tactile program | 10 minutes |

(identifying small objects by touch)

10:30	Sequence 4	
	Crawl	2 minutes
	Creep	2 minutes
	Roll and somersault	1 minute
	Brachiate	1 minute
	Hang upside down	1 minute

154

10:45   Sequence 5
        Crawl   2 minutes
        Creep   2 minutes
        Roll and somersault   1 minute
        Brachiate   1 minute
        Hang upside down   1 minute

11:00   Sequence 6
        Crawl   2 minutes
        Creep   2 minutes
        Roll and somersault   1 minute
        Brachiate   1 minute
        Hang upside down   1 minute

11:15   Sequence 7
        Crawl   2 minutes
        Creep   2 minutes
        Roll and somersault   1 minute
        Brachiate   1 minute
        Hang upside down   1 minute

11:30   Sequence 8
        Crawl   2 minutes
        Creep   2 minutes
        Roll and somersault   1 minute
        Brachiate   1 minute
        Hang upside down   1 minute

11:45   Sequence 9
        Crawl   2 minutes
        Creep   2 minutes
        Roll and somersault   1 minute
        Brachiate   1 minute
        Hang upside down   1 minute

12:00	Lunch	1 hour
1:00	Sequence 10	
	Crawl	2 minutes
	Creep	2 minutes
	Roll and somersault	1 minute
	Brachiate	1 minute
	Hang upside down	1 minute
1:15	Sequence 11	
	Crawl	2 minutes
	Creep	2 minutes
	Roll and somersault	1 minute
	Brachiate	1 minute
	Hang upside down	1 minute
1:30	Third patterning	5 minutes
	Crawl	5 minutes
	Creep	5 minutes
	Brachiate	1 minute
	Hang upside down	1 minute
	Roll and somersault	1 minute
	Eye exercise	5 minutes
2:00	Fourth patterning	5 minutes
	Crawl	5 minutes
	Creep	5 minutes
	Brachiate	1 minute
	Hang upside down	1 minute
	Roll and somersault	1 minute
	Eye exercises	5 minutes
2:30	Sequence 12	
	Crawl	2 minutes
	Creep	2 minutes

	Roll and somersault	1 minute
	Brachiate	1 minute
	Hang upside down	1 minute

2:45   Sequence 13

	Crawl	2 minutes
	Creep	2 minutes
	Roll and somersault	1 minute
	Brachiate	1 minute
	Hang upside down	1 minute

3:00   Eye exercise   10 minutes

3:10   Reading program   10 minutes

3:20   Tactile program   10 minutes

3:30   Sequence 14

	Crawl	2 minutes
	Creep	2 minutes
	Roll and somersault	1 minute
	Brachiate	1 minute
	Hang upside down	1 minute

3:45   Sequence 15

	Crawl	2 minutes
	Creep	2 minutes
	Roll and somersault	1 minute
	Brachiate	1 minute
	Hang upside down	1 minute

4:00   Sequence 16

	Crawl	2 minutes
	Creep	2 minutes
	Roll and somersault	1 minute

| | Brachiate | 1 minute |
| | Hang upside down | 1 minute |

4:15	Sequence 17	
	Crawl	2 minutes
	Creep	2 minutes
	Roll and somersault	1 minute
	Brachiate	1 minute
	Hang upside down	1 minute

4:30	Sequence 18	
	Crawl	2 minutes
	Creep	2 minutes
	Roll and somersault	1 minute
	Brachiate	1 minute
	Hang upside down	1 minute

5:00	Bath	15 minutes
5:30	Dinner	1 hour
6:30	Free time	1 hour
7:30	Bed	

"As you can see," Dad told us, "this isn't something that will take a few minutes of your mother's time. It is an all-out program which has to be done every day. It is going to involve some of my time in the evenings and on weekends. And it will involve much of your time, too. If we do this program, it's going to take all of us to get it done.

Your mother will need your help, more than ever before, with the housework. And there will be parts of the program which you can help with.

"If this were going to take only a week or so, then we might say, 'like it or not, we're going to do it, so everyone chip in,'" he said. "But it doesn't look like a couple of weeks will do the trick for Jeremiah—maybe more like a couple of years, if we're lucky. If we're not lucky, maybe more. The Chair is open to comments."

"Mr. Chairman!"

"The Chair recognizes Josh."

"Are you sure we have to do all of the program every day?"

"You heard what they said at The Institutes."

"Yes," Josh said, "but how do we know they really mean it? I mean, how do we know it doesn't really take half as much of this stuff to make him well and they're telling us to do double so they make sure we do enough?"

"Oh, Josh," I groaned.

"Don't you 'Oh, Josh' me," he grumbled. "Coach Willoughby does that all the time. He says, 'You guys run two miles every day.' But we know that he's happy if we run a mile."

"The whole world isn't a 3-2 League," I informed him. "And not everybody threatens people like Coach Willoughby does."

"Yeah?" Josh replied. "Says you. But how do we know?"

"We don't know." Mother said, "but how

would you like to stake Jeremiah's life on supposes?"

Josh thought about it for a moment. "I wouldn't," he answered.

I spoke up. "I don't know why we're talking about it. All of you know as well as I do that we're going to do it. It's like Mr. Doman told us. If a family was going on a picnic and as they were leaving their house, one little kid fell down and cut his knee, the dad would say, 'Sorry, kids, but we got to get him to the hospital and get his knee sewed up; the picnic will have to wait.'"

"But our picnics are going to have an awful long wait," Dad reasoned.

"Then they will just have to wait," I told him.

"Besides," Josh said, "who wants to go on a picnic if Jeremiah doesn't get better? It would be more fun if he could take care of himself."

We voted. The program won.

Both Josh's and my words had been loaded with self-sacrifice and noble thoughts. In the following months, we would often be aware that noble words come easier than noble deeds; we would also learn that two years is a long time between picnics.

A Beehive

Dad had one more week of his vacation remaining. During that week, the inside of our house was changed in so many ways that it was unbelievable. By the end of the week, if someone had brought me inside and asked me to tell him where we were, I don't think I would have recognized our own house.

Dad and Josh built the patterning table, and I helped Dad construct the overhead ladder. The furniture had to be moved out and the patterning table and overhead ladder moved in. What had once been our family room now looked more like a room for therapy.

Since Jeremiah was to crawl and creep on both textured and smooth surfaces, we arranged the furniture in the living room and the dining room so he would have a clear throughway. The carpet in the living room would provide the textured surface; the floor tile in the kitchen would provide the smooth. Because he would be able to crawl from the living room, through the kitchen and the dining room, and through the living room again without stopping or turning around, that route soon became known in our home as "the loop."

Since the closet in my bedroom was bigger than the one in Josh's, I lost half of mine. A completely dark place was needed so Mother could do a series of eye exercises with Jeremiah; she had been instructed to flash lights in his eyes in a darkened room. So one half of my closet held dresses, shoes, and coats; the other half had different kinds of lights and switches installed. It was a psychedelic closet if there every was one. (My friends thought it was really neat; I should have charged admission.)

During that week, much of Mother's time was spent on the telephone calling friends to tell them about the program and that we needed people to help pattern Jeremiah. Mom and Dad had decided that although we might be able to do the patternings ourselves, we should have volunteers. With volunteers the patternings could be done during the day which meant that we would not have to do them at night or wait until at least three of us were at home. There was also an advantage in having other people know how to pattern in case any of us became sick for a day or two.

162

Since three people were required to do a patterning and we were to allow at least thirty minutes between each patterning, Mother decided we should have two teams for each day—a morning team and an afternoon team. The morning team would complete one patterning, wait thirty minutes, and then do a second one. The afternoon teams would do the same.

Mother felt it might be too difficult to get the same six people to come to our house every day, so she decided to get six people for Monday, another six for Tuesday, and so on. Multiply six people by seven days in the week—forty-two people; we needed forty-two people. We weren't sure we even knew forty-two people well enough to ask them to help. It soon became clear then that we would have to ask people whom we didn't know well enough.

Mother placed an ad in the paper.

> People needed to pattern brain-injured boy.
> Please phone 584-9023.

We were not sure many people would understand the ad, but Mrs. Tyson at The Institutes had told us that because of the many magazine articles and books written on the subject, a great many people would recognize the term "patterning." She was right. As soon as the ad appeared in the paper, we began to receive calls from people who wished to volunteer. By the end of the week we had twenty-eight people and more calls were coming in each day.

During all of the activities and the preparations, Jeremiah watched with great interest. Although we kept telling him that these things were for him, I don't think he really understood what we were doing. In fact he may have thought we had all lost our senses. After all, who in his right mind would build a padded table and tell a five-year-old kid that it was for him? I think he had every reason to question the state of our sanity.

We Begin

The first week of the program was both the easiest and the hardest. It was the easiest because it was all new and different, so it was exciting. Perhaps it seems more fun in memory than it was in reality. However, for me it was fun to see the patterners come for the first time and to find that after only a few minutes of instructions they could learn to pattern.

At the same time, it may have been one of the most difficult weeks because everything was new and different—and at times, Jeremiah could really be a stinker.

The first two teams were the hardest hit. Jeremiah decided to display his capacity for crying and screaming much as he had done at The Institutes. At home it was really much worse because the volunteers were so afraid they might hurt him. Even if he had been an absolute dream and kept his mouth shut they would probably have been nervous, but with him bellowing and carrying on so, I would not have been surprised if some of the women had left never to come back.

But they had stout hearts and weathered the storms.

I think it was during the third patterning that Jeremiah either wore himself out or decided that he might as well give in. I never will forget it. Right in the middle of a good cry, he gave a sudden sigh and relaxed. My heart leaped into my throat. At first, he looked so peaceful I thought he had died.

Art Sandler had told us that some kids actually go to sleep while they are being patterned, but as far as I know Jeremiah never did. From that time on, however, he never seemed to mind being patterned. In fact, he really seemed to enjoy the new people coming in to see him. I think he liked the attention.

Some of the people who came to pattern him would either tell us on the phone, or at the door before they came in, that they had come only for the one time, and that they could not be *regulars.* But after they had patterned him once, usually they signed up as regular patterners. Mother said she thought they told us that before just in case they found that Jeremiah was terribly deformed or that they couldn't learn to pattern. I think she was right. I think they had every right to be cautious because the program was so new to them.

What happened was that they fell in love with my little brother, which didn't surprise me one bit.

I remember one older woman who looked very stern. She had white hair and walked like a four-star general. You know the type. I'm not sure why she happened to come in the first place. Perhaps she was from one of the women's clubs. Anyway, she came to the door and announced to my mother before entering that she could help "only this once."

She hardly spoke to the other people and she glanced around the house as if she was looking down her nose at everyone and everything.

At a safe distance, where she couldn't hear, I told Josh that I thought "Mrs. Snooty" would be a good name for her.

Josh said he thought "Mrs. Sourpuss" would be better. For once I agreed with him.

As I remember, she was on Jeremiah's right side at the patterning table and she had a great deal of difficulty keeping in rhythm with the other people. Mother had to stop them several times and they had to begin again. Although the woman said nothing, I could see that she didn't like the interruptions.

Mother finally gritted her teeth and let them finish although it wasn't a good patterning.

As soon as they stopped, Jeremiah sat up on the table and looked up at the woman.

"What's name?" he asked.

"What?" she said, as if she smelled something bad.

"He wants to know your name," Mother told her.

She looked down at Jeremiah. "Mrs. Roberts," she said.

"First name?" he wanted to know.

"Bessy," she told him, not cracking even a hint of a smile.

Jeremiah stood up and to everyone's surprise reached out and put his arms around her neck.

"I like Bessy," he said hugging her.

I thought for a moment that she was going to cry. Tears came to her eyes and finally she couldn't hold back any longer—she *smiled!*

"Well, I like you too, honey," she replied.

"Carry me," he said.

"What?" She didn't understand.

"Some of the patterners have been carrying him into the living room so he can start crawling, but you don't have to," Mother told her.

"Of course Bessy will carry him," she said picking him up. "Well, I haven't seen such a friendly child since I don't know when."

That was the end of "Mrs. Sourpuss" and the beginning of "Aunt" Bessy. She became a regular on Wednesday mornings. Sometimes she came by during the week to see if she could help in some other way.

Josh never told Mom and Dad about the "Mrs. Sourpuss" and neither did I.

It seems that Jeremiah had the best idea; he simply charmed her.

I was scheduled as a regular on the Saturday morning team and on the Sunday afternoon team. Josh was on the Sunday morning team. We both filled in for people who were absent for one reason or the other.

Josh saw it as a way of building up the muscles in his arms, so he rarely complained when he was asked to be a substitute.

I looked at patterning in an entirely different way. Mother always says that I'm her dramatic one. Well, maybe I am. I could not forget what Glenn Doman had told us. He said, "Patterning shows the child how it feels to crawl properly. The patterners are programming the child's brain."

Then he said the part that always makes chills go up and down my spine. "A surgical team, during open brain surgery, must have four qualities: one, every member has to be highly skilled at what he is doing; two, they have to work skillfully together; three, they have to be able to work hard physically; and four, they're working with the child's brain to save his life. They are doing *open* brain surgery.

"A patterning team has these very same qualities," he said. One, every member on the team has to be highly skilled at what he is doing; two, they have to work skillfully together; three, they have to be able to work hard physically; and four, they are working with the child's brain to

169

save his life. They are doing *closed* brain surgery."

That closed brain surgery line sounded spooky and wonderful. Every time I was at the patterning table, I thought about it. I imagined that all those billions of brain cells which were inside Jeremiah's head were tiny lights. As we patterned, I thought about them coming on one at a time—one light here, another light there, and in the distance still another one lighting up.

Sometimes I wondered how many lights it would take, how many brain cells would have to be activated before we would see a difference in Jeremiah.

Would it take a hundred?

Would it take a thousand?

Or maybe a million?

Or a billion?

If it took a billion, how many patternings would be necessary to turn on those billion lights?

How many miles would Jeremiah have to crawl and how many miles would he have to creep before the neons came on?

How long would it take to make one little miracle?

A Phone Call from a Stranger

By the second week, the ads which Mother had placed in the newspaper and the calls she had made brought us close to the forty-two people we needed. We had so many calls that one of our biggest problems soon became answering the telephone. It seemed that before we turned around from one call, it would ring again. In the beginning this was exactly what we had prayed for. But since the Lord knew how busy we were, we hoped he might have arranged for the calls to come between patternings or after Josh and I had finished our homework.

Although we sometimes found ourselves complaining under our breaths, we were really grateful for the calls. We really needed people.

"Hello, I'm a friend of the Davises and Mrs. Davis told me that you need someone to help with your little boy," a caller might begin.

171

Some of the calls were from friends of the Joneses, the MacElhaneys, the Raffertys, or of people we didn't even know.

"Hello, I read in the newspaper that you needed help. Could you use me on Tuesday mornings?"

Everything was going along better than we had hoped for. We were getting enough people and we were beginning to adjust ourselves to the hectic schedule of so many people coming in and out of our house. Then one night the telephone rang.

I answered the phone. "Hello."

"May I speak to Mrs. Rodgers?" the voice said.

"I'm sorry," I replied, "but she is busy now. May I take a message or have her call you back?"

"Tell her it's important that I talk to her," the voice insisted.

"But she's doing therapy with my little brother now and can't come to the phone," I told her. "If you'll give me your number..."

"No," the voice interrupted, "you tell her that I know all about that therapy and know that it doesn't work. You're wasting your time."

"Who is this?" I asked.

"Never mind," the voice replied. "You tell her what I said."

"Wait, don't hang up," I urged. "Wait a minute and I'll get my mother."

I ran into the bedroom where she was doing an eye exercise with Jeremiah and told her about the call. By the time Mother got to the phone the woman had hung up.

"Don't worry about it, M.J.," Mother told me. "The woman must be emotionally unbalanced. It was just a crank. She won't call back."

"But what if she was telling the truth?" I said.

"If what she said were true, then she would have waited for me to come to the phone, and she would not have minded giving her name."

I agreed. But when Mother walked into the bedroom, I couldn't help but look at the phone for a moment and wonder if the woman might sometime call again.

The Everyday Schedule

By September, when Josh and I went back to school, Jeremiah had been on the program for six weeks. There was little which was new or different. It hadn't taken us very long to realize that every day at home was pretty much the same.

Mother and Jeremiah's lives were lived by the schedule. They woke by the schedule. They ate by the schedule. He was patterned by the schedule. He crawled by the schedule. He crept by the schedule. And when at last the program was completed, Jeremiah was bathed and put to bed by the schedule.

For Josh and me, school provided a means of escape. Dad's work, too, took him away from home. But there was no way that Mother could leave the routine. And, of course, the program couldn't be done without Jeremiah. So he and Mother had little time for a recess or a coffee break.

174

I remember that during the first days, some of the things Jeremiah had to do looked like fun to him. When Josh or I got down on the floor and crawled or crept with him, it all seemed like a game. But soon, very soon, Josh and I learned that crawling on our stomachs for more than a few minutes was not a game; it was hard work. And it didn't take long for Jeremiah to discover the same thing.

On some days he would crawl when he was told. Some days he had to be coaxed. Sometimes he had to be threatened. And there were times when Mother had to use a switch. But that was not often, thank goodness.

When Josh and I got home from school, we could tell pretty well how the day had gone. If Mother greeted us with a broad smile on her face, we knew that the patterners had come on time and that Jeremiah had done as he was told. But if she met us with a cloud of gloom hanging above her head, we knew all had not gone well.

Many nights, supper had not been started. We had hamburgers more often than roast or something that required time or attention. For the duration of the program, we said good-bye to homemade pies and pastries. Our kitchen was run like a "Shop and Go."

In self-defense, I started to learn to cook. In defense of the family, we kept plenty of Alka Seltzer in the cabinet. I began washing the evening dishes and, with much protest, Josh dried them. We both had to make our own beds in the morning, and I ran the sweeper and dusted the furniture on Saturdays. Josh emptied the trash. Sometimes I watched Jeremiah crawl and creep so Mother could start dinner. Sometimes Josh would watch him.

Josh and I didn't do all of these things because we were told that we had to, and we didn't do these things because we were "goody-two-shoes." We did them because the evenings went better if we did.

I think we became aware that when Mother was tired and there were dishes stacked in the kitchen and the beds were unmade, she would be very nervous and irritable. As she said, "Sometimes the walls close in." I knew what she meant by that, because sometimes when I have put off homework until the last night, I have had the walls close in on me, too.

Needless to say, in those first months we were under a great deal of pressure. The worst pressure of all was the wondering if the program were going to work. Sometimes I saw Dad studying Jeremiah's appearance, trying to see if he could detect a difference. If he noticed that I saw him, he quickly looked the other way—and I pretended I hadn't noticed. I saw Mom do the same thing.

We played this game because we were afraid to let our fears be seen or discussed.

"Boy, Jeremiah sure looks better today," I would say in a bright and cheerful voice.

"Sure does," Dad or Mom would answer.

"Looks like a real winner," Josh would chime in.

I don't think any one of us believed what the others were saying any more than we meant what we said, but it was better than sitting around with down-at-the-mouth expressions on our faces and feeling sorry for ourselves.

All the time we watched and waited for that one spark of hope. We waited for Jeremiah to do one thing—anything—that would show us something was happening inside his little head.

We worked and we waited.

The Stranger Calls Again

I recognized the voice the minute I heard it.

"May I speak to Mrs. Rodgers, please?" the voice said in exactly the same tones as before.

"One moment," I said, trying not to reveal my excitement.

"Hssssst," I signaled to Mother as I covered the mouthpiece of the telephone with my hand. "It's *her.*"

"Who?" Mother asked, then realized who before I answered.

"Hello," Mother said, taking the phone.

"Yes, this is Mrs. Rodgers," I heard her say. "Yes, we have a little boy on a therapy program.... What? Who is this? And how do you know that it doesn't work? And where was that? New Orleans? And what were *their* names? Mr. and Mrs. William Landers? And what is their child's name? Alice. Who is this? Why won't you tell me your name? Hello? Hello?"

Mother looked at me. "She hung up."

"What did she say?" I asked.

"She said that she patterned a little girl in New Orleans before she moved here and the child showed no improvement; instead she got worse."

"Do you believe that?" I asked.

"I don't know what to believe," Mother said quietly.

When Dad came home, Mother told him about the caller.

"Do you think it's true?" Mother asked, trying not to show how worried she really was.

"There's one way to find out," he said.

Dad walked over to the telephone and dialed for long distance information. "Operator, would you please give me the number in New Orleans for a Mr. William Landers? No, I don't know his address.... Is that right? Then give me both of them."

After jotting the numbers on a piece of paper, Dad told us the operator had found two William Landers listed.

He dialed the first number.

A woman answered.

"Hello," Dad said, "is this Mrs. Landers?"

"Do you have a little girl named Alice? I see. I'm sorry to bother you. I must have the wrong number."

He dialed the second number.

This time a man answered.

"Mr. Landers?" Dad said. "Do you have a little

girl named Alice? I see. Sorry to have bothered you. I have the wrong number."

Mother drew a sigh of relief. "The woman was lying," she said. "She must be very sick to do such a thing."

Dad didn't answer; he sat very still, thinking.

"There is one possibility I hadn't thought of," he said finally.

"What's that?" Mother asked.

Without answering, Dad picked up the phone and dialed information again.

"Operator, in New Orleans, do you have a *Bill* Landers listed? You do. Will you give the number please? Thank you."

"But she said *William*," Mother insisted.

"I know," Dad replied. "She may have assumed he was listed as William. But some Williams prefer Bill."

Dad started to dial the number.

"Don't do it," Mother said suddenly.

Dad stopped dialing and looked at her curiously.

"Don't call," she said. "I don't want to know about an Alice Landers who has—or has not—been on the program. I don't want to talk about it anymore. I just want to forget that that woman ever called here."

"But you won't forget it," Dad said.

"Yes, I will," Mother answered quickly.

Dad looked at her in a very straight way.

"No, I won't," she finally admitted. "But I don't want to know."

"Helen," Dad said, "no matter what the truth happens to be, it can't possibly be as bad as our wondering about it."

"All right," Mother agreed. "Go on and call."

Dad dialed the number.

A woman answered.

"May I speak to Mrs. Landers?" he asked.

"This is she."

"Mrs. Landers, do you have a little girl named Alice?"

After a long pause the woman asked "Why do you want to know?"

"My name is John Rodgers," he told her. "We live in Indianapolis. We have a little boy who is brain-injured and is on a therapy program. A woman has called here a couple of times and refused to give her name, but she told us she knows this therapy will not help our little boy because she personally knew of an Alice Landers who was on a similar program and..."

"Mr. Rodgers," the woman interrupted, "my daughter's name is Alice and she was on this program."

"Was she helped by the program?" he asked.

"Not much," she answered.

"I see," my father said quietly.

"But it had nothing to do with the program," she added, "because we didn't do it very long—only three or four weeks."

181

"May I ask why?"

"Yes," she said slowly. "We were in an automobile accident—and our little girl, Alice, was killed."

"Mrs. Landers, I'm terribly sorry to hear that," my father said gently. "I'm sorry to have troubled you with this phone call."

"That's quite all right," she said.

"Do you have any idea who this woman is or why she has been calling us?" he asked.

"I have no idea," she answered.

"Can you think of anyone who helped with your program who has since moved to Indianapolis?"

"No, but I can make some inquiries if you wish to see if I can find out."

"We would appreciate that," Dad told her.

After Dad gave her our telephone number, he thanked her and hung up the phone.

Since Mother and I had heard most of the conversation, there was little for him to tell us.

"Why do you suppose anyone would do such a thing?" Mother said, thinking aloud.

"Beats me," Dad said, shaking his head slowly.

Whenever I think about those phone calls and that night, I still get a tight feeling in my ~~stomache~~ stomach. For a long time after that when we were downtown or in the supermarket, I ~~would~~ sometimes looked at women and wondered if one of them had been the caller. I wondered if we ever saw her, or if she ever saw us. It was a most uneasy feeling to realize that she might recognize us, but we wouldn't know who she was. We hoped that we would never find out who she was.

Hotdogs and Cranberry Sauce

"The program must be done every day—Monday, Tuesday, Wednesday, Thanksgiving...."

Thanksgiving.

Mother had decided that program or no program, we were going to have an old-fashioned Thanksgiving dinner—baked turkey, dressing, cranberry sauce, pumpkin pie—the works.

The only thing required to produce this piece of magic was a foolproof schedule. She figured that if we canceled the afternoon patterning, got up at six in the morning to do the afternoon patternings then, and if Dad took over the morning programs, she could prepare the dinner.

The schedule was arranged with the precision of clockwork. Nothing had been left to chance—well, almost nothing. How did we know it was going to be called the year of the London flu?

The night before Thanksgiving, Mother had a slight fever, but by morning it had soared to 104 degrees and her body ached all over. We had lost our cook.

Dad refused to accept defeat. He decided that if Josh and I would take over some of the programs, *he* would cook the dinner.

So we gave it a try.

By ten o'clock, Dad put the turkey in the oven.

By eleven o'clock, he too had a headache.

By twelve o'clock, Dad's fever matched Mom's.

At about one o'clock, we discovered that he had forgotten to turn on the oven.

At 1:05, Dad went to bed.

After Josh and I finished Jeremiah's program, we fixed hot dogs and had a little cranberry sauce for dessert.

If the Pilgrim fathers' dinner hadn't turned out any better, I'm sure they would have sailed straight back to England.

That night after we had gone to bed, I lay there thinking about the events of the day. Then an awful thought crossed my mind: What if the therapy was working and what if Jeremiah's brain was soaking up the information? If it was, I thought, maybe he thinks Thanksgiving is a time when your parents get sick and you eat hot dogs and cranberry sauce.

A Pleasant Surprise

For some reason we expected to see differences in Jeremiah's physical abilities before we noticed mental changes. (It seems that I had not learned my lesson from Harold and Jimmy completely.)

When Mother began the reading program with Jeremiah, she didn't really believe that he would be able to catch on. Even though Mr. Doman's book stressed that reading a word with one's eyes was no more difficult than hearing a word with one's ears, we still had this idea in our heads that reading was a difficult skill which could be learned only after hours and hours of study and tedium. Since there were only fifteen minutes each day alloted to Jeremiah's reading program, we assumed it would be months before he would get the idea that the words really meant something.

As we were instructed, we printed the words in big red letters on large cards. The first word was *Mom*. The second was *Dad*. After those we printed parts of the body—*arm, leg, hand, foot,* and so on. We printed words for objects which are in our house: *floor, door, chair, table*—all the words for things that Jeremiah had seen every day and words that he had heard time and time again.

He surprised us. The first day he seemed to get the idea that *Mom* was Mom. The second day he seemed to understand that *Dad* was Dad. After a couple of weeks, he recognized the words *toes, knee, elbow, arm, leg, head, chair, table, door.* Jeremiah could read over twenty-five words. We were both surprised and delighted. And we were proud!

A Very Merry

Christmas!

Never before in his life had Jeremiah given the slightest hint that he knew who Santa Claus was or what Christmas was all about. We had long before given up taking him to a department store to sit on Santa's lap because such trips had meant nothing but screaming and crying. Worse than that, Jeremiah just never seemed to understand about gifts and giving. Since some of the toys he had received had frightened him, we had to be very careful about what we bought for him.

However, this year he loved looking at the lights on the Christmas tree and seemed to enjoy the colorful packages. On Christmas morning he unwrapped his presents and was very happy to find the toys in the boxes.

When I asked him if he knew where they had come from, he quickly answered, "Santa Claus."

"How do you know that?" I asked.

I should have guessed the answer.

"Charlie told me."

A Good Report

January 14—Jeremiah had been on the program for six months and, to our surprise, we were all surviving. The time had passed more quickly than we had thought it would. And the time had come for Dad and Mom to take him back to The Institutes for his first reevaluation.

It had been decided that since Josh and I were in school, we would not go with them. Grandmother Rodgers came from Chicago to stay with us.

As the car pulled out of the driveway that morning, we waved good-bye. No sooner had the car turned the corner than I felt terribly lonely. I think Josh felt the same.

It wasn't that we didn't enjoy having Grandmother Rodgers with us, because we did. She was a lot of fun to be with, and besides, we hadn't seen her since before Jeremiah had gone on the program. It was a welcome time. It promised to be a week of homemade pies and cakes and all kinds of goodies that we had missed in the last six

189

months. During that week I gained six pounds and Josh had a stomachache twice.

Josh and I counted the days. We were eager to hear how the staff members at The Institutes had evaluated Jeremiah's progress. We hoped that they would be as pleased as we were. Although we realized he still had a long, long way to go before he was completely well, we felt that he had made a pretty good start.

He was now crawling in a good cross-pattern.

He could now creep in an *almost* good cross-pattern.

He could feed himself. (He was still slow, but not nearly so messy.)

He didn't drool nearly as much.

His left eye now seemed to move better with the right eye.

And he could read over forty words.

In fact, we thought he was a little better in every way.

When Mother called, she told us that our evaluations of his progress had been pretty good, because the staff members at The Institutes had said almost the same thing—except for reading. It seems that they tested his reading late in the day and Jeremiah had decided to be contrary.

When they showed him the word *Dad* he said that it was *horse*. When they showed him the word *arm*, he said it was *leg*. When they showed him the word *chair*, he said it was *table* and so on.

Mother told us that they would stay the full

week and be given additional programs and instructions. They would be home the following Sunday as planned.

While they were gone, it seemed strange to walk through the house. It was so quiet. There were no patterners at the table; no one was doing an eye exercise in my closet; no one was crawling around "the loop." It didn't seem like our house at all. But I knew, and the house seemed to sense it too, that in a short time it would once again be like a three-ring circus.

The Days Grow Long

The following Monday we were in business again. The patterners were eager to know how Jeremiah had done and were happy to learn of his progress.

Although I saw that Mother was pleased to tell them of the improvements, I could tell she wished those improvements were greater than they had been. I would not have mentioned it to her or anyone else, but I had hoped Jeremiah's progress would be better too. I guess we wanted a faster miracle.

As we started the new programs with Jeremiah, we were also given a new set of goals. Within the next six months Jeremiah was supposed to be able to do the following things: read simple sentences; run in a good cross-pattern, completely undress himself, speak in short sentences, and print his own name.

To most people those things are simple, but for Jeremiah to be able to do any of them meant he would have to improve a lot.

I thought the first six months of the program would be the hardest part and that it would be easier after that. That surely wasn't the case. If anything, the new program required even more time and patience.

We had passed the stage of wondering if we could do the program or not because we had done it. We were seasoned veterans. Now we wondered how much longer Jeremiah could take the every-day pressure and strain.

There was so little time for him to play or do anything that he might want to do. There wasn't even time for him to sit and look out the window.

When I stop to think of it, Jeremiah certainly never had much of a childhood—at least not one that anyone could count. He had never ridden his tricycle down the sidewalk. He had never been allowed to be out of our yard without holding onto one of our hands. He had never played hopscotch or pin-the-tail-on-the-donkey. He had never bought anything. He had never counted the pennies in his piggy bank. Even if he were told how many pennies he had, it would not have meant anything to him. We might just as well have told him how many miles it was to the moon.

If early some morning Jeremiah had walked through the house screaming and had never stopped, I would not have been surprised. After all, following a ten-hour program every day is a lot to expect from a little kid. Right? Right!

However, Jeremiah seemed to take the program as a way of life that was not to be questioned. Oh, there were times that he griped and fussed about it, but he never seemed to question whether we loved him or not. Maybe that's because so often we told him we did.

I might say, "Come on, Jeremiah, crawl for me."

And if he asked why, I'd answer, "Because I love you."

"Okay," he would reply and get down and crawl.

Or Mother might say, Jeremiah, be more careful when you're eating and don't spill so much food."

If he asked why, she would answer, "Because I love you."

Actually we were telling him the truth. We were doing the program because we loved him. I don't think we could have found a better reason to give him.

It occurred to me one day that families are lifetime things. We can choose who our friends are, but when it comes to brothers or sisters, there is no choice. We take what we get -- like it or lump it.

Friends may move away and we sometimes

lose track of acquaintances, but a brother is a brother for all of life.

I once once read that our spirits were allowed to select a family before birth. I don't know if that's true or not, but I wish it were. I think it is a really neat idea. I would like to think that Jeremiah's spirit looked all over the earth until he found us, and he said to himself, "Since I'm going to need a lot of help, I had better take that family, because the parents are strong people and the brother and sister are understanding. Yes, the family on Maple Street — the Rodgers — will do just fine."

When I think of it in that way, I get goose pimples all over because it's so lovely and spooky.

Oh, Jeremiah, you just <u>have</u> to get well!

How Interesting!

Some people thought our home situation was not only a strange one for Jeremiah but for Josh and me too. Well, I suppose it was. Yet when I looked around me, I noticed that many of my friends had just as strange setups at their houses—well, almost, anyway.

For instance, Martha Rountree's parents were getting a divorce and both of them wanted her to live with them. Karen Lewis's parents were divorcing and neither one wanted her to live with them, so she was being shipped off to a grandmother in Pineville, Arkansas. Robert Miller's parents drank a lot. Jonathan Abbot's parents never knew where he was or what kind of trouble he would be into next. When I think about some of the others and compare, I don't think that Josh and I had it so bad.

On the other hand, everything at our house wasn't peaches and cream. No matter how much we loved Jeremiah, we still got tired of *seeing, hearing, feeling, smelling,* and *tasting* the program every day. It was the sameness, the sameness, the sameness that wore us down.

Other kids could come home to their parents and ask, "Hey, can we go to a movie this weekend?" All their parents had to think about was whether or not they had recently been to too many films or to check the parental guidance ratings. However, if Josh or I wanted to go somewhere, our parents had also to figure out if they could arrange to drive us there between patternings and if one of them could pick us up.

Everything had to be time-slotted. Nothing was simple, like open house at school. First Mother was going to finish the program and Dad was going to the open house. Then Dad said he thought that Mom should go because she had not been out of the house in several days. He said he would finish the program. So Mom agreed and went in to take a shower and get ready. It was almost eight o'clock when one of us realized that she had not come out of the bedroom. When we looked in we found that she had lain down on the bed for a minute to rest and had fallen asleep. None of us had the heart to waken her, so neither of them went to open house.

The next day my teacher said she had missed seeing my parents the night before. Maybe she didn't mean anything by it, but it seemed to me that she implied they weren't interested in what was going on at school. I started to explain how busy they were but stopped. It had to be seen to be believed.

When my girl friends came home from school with me, they were always interested in what new things we were doing with Jeremiah and how he was getting along. None of them—*absolutely none*—ever came in and looked down their noses at him or at us. I simply don't have friends like that.

On occasion a new friend would come to the house, and if by some miracle she hadn't heard about Jeremiah or the program, she might walk through the house and look around as one might survey the landscape of the moon or some other strange place.

The first time Lisa Allen came to my house, she looked around like that. When she saw all the patterners she asked if we had company or if we had a large family. I told her that they helped us with my brother's program.

"What kind of program?" she wanted to know.

"He's brain-injured," I told her.

"How interesting," she said.

Most of my friends thought it was *interesting*. Some of them were even on patterning teams.

Josh's friends were much the same. They all liked Jeremiah and were interested in his getting well.

One of the other mothers at The Institutes had told my parents that some of the kids at school teased her children about the condition of their sister. They called her a *mental retard* and called the other kids names. That never happened to us. It's a good thing, too. Neither Josh nor I would have put up with such attitudes. Any kid dumb enough to mouth off about Jeremiah would have been asking for a bruised lip or a black eye. (Maybe I shouldn't have written that because I really don't believe in physical violence—well, not most of the time; however, Josh does. I must admit there are times when it saves a lot of explaining.)

I suppose during all of this, Josh and I missed our parents most of all. There simply weren't enough hours for them to work, do the program, and spend very much time with us. Sometimes if we asked for help with our homework or if we needed to talk to them about some minor problems, we had to wait. Quite often after we had waited and finally sat down to talk, they were so exhausted we weren't sure they heard our questions.

Sometimes after we had gone to bed, Mom would come in and sit down for a few minutes.

"Is everything all right?" she would ask.

"Okay."

"Everything going all right at school?"

"Fine."

Big Hopes—Little Changes

Although we watched for changes in Jeremiah, they were so subtle and developed so gradually that when they occurred we found we had taken them for granted.

One morning Jeremiah came into my room, pulled at the bedcovers, and said, "M.J., wake up! Wake up!"

"Go away," I groaned.

"I will not go away. Wake up," he insisted.

"What do you want?" I asked.

"Will you tie my shoe?" he asked.

"Later."

"Please?"

"Tie it yourself," I told him.

"I can't," he answered.

"Try," I ordered.

"I did," he said.

"Try again!"

"I can't," he insisted.

"Why not?"

"Because I can't get my damned fingers to work right," he explained.

"Jeremiah!" I exclaimed. "What did you say?"

He repeated his statement stubbornly, "I can't get my damned fingers to work right."

"How would you like to have your mouth washed out with soap? I scolded.

"No!" he said. "It wouldn't taste good."

"Well, then you stop saying *damn.*"

"Okay," he replied, climbing up on the bed. "Will you tie my shoe—*please!*"

So I tied his shoestrings. Then he jumped down and started to run out of the room.

"What do you say?" I reminded him.

"You always say thank you," he said mechanically (he had been told a thousand times), then he added, "and you don't say *damn.*"

I couldn't help but laugh. Then I began to consider the conversation we had just had. I realized that it had, indeed, been a conversation. It had been an exchange of ideas and an explanation of wants and needs. And Jeremiah had spoken in complete sentences. Jeremiah was really talking.

How long had he been doing this, I wondered. Had it started that morning? Or had he been doing it for several weeks without our realizing it? Perhaps we were too busy looking for changes to recognize them when they happened.

Later that morning I mentioned the conversation to Mother. I soon found out that I wasn't as observant as I thought; she had noticed the improvement several weeks before.

As we came to the end of the first year of Jeremiah's program, we could see several improvements. He had stopped drooling. His walking had greatly improved. He didn't fall as often. His eye was straighter.

His speech was much better, but it was still difficult to understand all the things he said. Members of our family could understand him. Many of the regular patterners could make out most of his words, but outsiders had to ask him to repeat. He didn't put clear beginnings and endings on words; he talked as if he had cotton in his mouth.

He had been absolutely right about his fingers. He still had problems feeding himself. It was hard for him to use crayons with much skill. Although he could now unbutton his clothes and undress himself, he still had to have help getting his arms into sleeves. When he tried to button his shirt or coat, he sometimes became so frustrated he cried. He simply could not get his fingers to work right.

Of course we knew that the problem was not his fingers. The problem was where it always had been—in his brain. More lights still needed to be turned on.

New Goals

The long cold winter finally gave way to spring, and summer followed soon after.

We had looked forward to the second week in July because that was the time we were to take Jeremiah back to The Institutes for another reevaluation. We were eager for them to see the improvements that he had made. We also hoped they might say he had done so well we might get an *easier* program.

Josh didn't go with us on this trip. Since his baseball team had honored him by making him captain, he simply couldn't desert his stouthearted men in their quest for glory on the field of fair play. Rah, rah, rah! Grandmother Rodgers came to stay with the 3-2 League's answer to Hank Aaron, while the rest of us headed east.

I was eager to see The Institutes again. The fact that Jimmy was going to be there had nothing to do with it—well, almost nothing.

Jimmy was six inches taller than he had been the year before and looked twice as much like David Cassidy. He no longer had *dyslexia*—I guess he didn't; he could read now. The best news of all: Jimmy had graduated from the program. All the parents in the waiting room congratulated him, and his parents were so happy.

Jimmy's graduation seemed to encourage the rest of us. It gave us hope that there was an end to the programs. I wished with all my heart that the end to Jeremiah's would come soon, but I knew he still had a long way to go.

That day Jeremiah was in a terrific mood. He was outgoing and friendly to everyone he saw. The evaluations went quickly and easily because he cooperated with everything that was asked of him.

Meg Tyson remembered the squirrel he had seen outside her window the first time we were there. While we were in her office this time she said, "Jeremiah, how would you like to go to the window and see if Charlie is outside?"

He looked up at her. "Charlie is not here," he replied.

"Where is Charlie?" she wanted to know.

"He is in Indianapolis," he answered.

"Is he?"

"I think so," he said, then he looked down at the floor for a moment. "Josh says..."

"What does Josh say?" she asked.

"Josh says that a cat ate him."

"Oh, no!" Mrs. Tyson exclaimed. "I don't believe that. Charlie was much too fast for a cat to catch him."

Jeremiah looked up at her and smiled. "I think so too," he said.

"Good afternoon, young man," Glenn Doman said, reaching out his hand to shake Jeremiah's. "It's good to see you again."

"It's good to see you, too," Jeremiah answered. Then he looked up at Mr. Doman and asked, "Have I ever seen you before?"

"It's been a long time," Mr. Doman said.

"I remember," Jeremiah said. "It was night and I was sleepy and you talked and talked and talked."

"Yep, that's me, kid," Mr. Doman laughed, "the late-night talker."

He welcomed the rest of us and we sat down.

"During this last year you people have done a great deal of work," he said. "It looks like you have come through with flying colors, except I notice one of you is missing."

Dad explained about our baseball captain.

"Now then," Mr. Doman said, "after looking at the comments made by the other staff members who have seen Jeremiah, it becomes obvious to me that we are not looking at the same Jeremiah Rodgers today that we were looking at this time last year. Last year we saw an extremely awkward little kid who had many problems. He had hearing problems, vision problems, and couldn't read. Numbers meant nothing to him. He didn't

206

walk very well. In fact we weren't sure that he knew what was going on in the room.

"Today that Jeremiah is gone," he exclaimed. "I see before me now a very bright-eyed little boy who talks and smiles a lot. I am told he can read. He can turn somersaults. He can brachiate. Don't you see, we can now talk about Jeremiah in terms of things he *can* do, instead of things that he can't."

Mother and Dad smiled.

"Most of this morning you and the staff have talked about these things. While I think they are very interesting, I would like to suggest that we talk about how Jeremiah will be next year. We certainly hope that there will be as many changes in him in the future as there have been in the past. In fact, I think we dare hope for more."

He paused for a moment. "You know," he said, "I believe in setting goals. If we don't set goals, we won't know when we have succeeded or when we have failed. One year ago you and I set a goal for Jeremiah. The goal was for him to be perfectly well. We didn't set a time limit; we just said sometime in the future. You understand that much of the world believes getting well is an impossible goal for a brain-injured child. We made it anyway. Jeremiah can do things today that he couldn't do last year, and some of those things seemed a little impossible then."

We agreed.

"If you don't mind," he continued, "the goal I would like to set is for Jeremiah to be well by this time next year. I think we should now concentrate on achieving that goal."

"Do you really think that can be done?" Mother asked.

"I don't know," Mr. Doman answered. "But I would certainly like to try for it, wouldn't you?"

"Yes," she nodded her head.

"I think we should start planning what we're going to do with Jeremiah when he is well. That may sound a bit crazy to you, but I think it's very practical. If I had said to you a year ago, 'Jeremiah is brain-injured and next year he will not be any better,' that would have influenced your planning. I assure you if you had treated him as if he would never be better, he would not have gotten better. He has done things this year that most brain-injured kids never get a chance to do. If we had agreed last year that he was dumb, we certainly wouldn't have tried to teach him to read, now would we? Of course not. We agreed that he was brain-injured and that he needed to be programmed. Part of that programming was reading.

"You see," he continued, "we will never have to worry anymore about someone calling Jeremiah dumb. No one would dare call someone who can read dumb."

Mother and Dad were all smiles.

"Mr. and Mrs. Rodgers, if you make Jeremiah well by this time next year, what are you going to do with him?"

"I guess we will do the same thing with him as

we would with any other well child," Mother answered.

"And what would that be?" he asked.

"We will get him ready for school," she said.

"I think that would be fair enough and a good idea," Mr. Doman said, nodding his head, "not because he will learn more at school than he could at home but because most well kids go to school, and we would like to see Jeremiah with the well kids. We should start thinking about the time when he is ready to go to school. I have every hope that we can make him ready for school during this next year, but I am not as hopeful that school will be ready for him."

"What do you mean?" Dad asked.

"I mean this," Mr. Doman replied. "Until a few years ago, no one even thought it was possible to fix a brain-injured kid and send him into a regular classroom. When we first started doing it, we ran into some trouble. Some of the school systems couldn't lose sight of the old labels. If children had ever been labeled 'mentally retarded' or 'cerebral palsied,' the school personnel wanted to put these kids back into a special class, even if they passed all kinds of tests which proved that they could do the work in a regular classroom."

"Is that really true?" Dad asked.

"Although it sounds crazy, it certainly is true," Mr. Doman answered. "They told parents that their kids were 'mentally retarded,' because it said so on their old records. When the parents reminded them of the improvements in test scores,

209

the school personnel acted as if those better scores were mistakes. Or they insisted that within a short period of time the children would once again be the way they used to be. Many of our parents fought these kinds of battles. At the very time when success should have been within their grasp, they were faced with failure. It was really frustrating to have a kid ready to go to school, able to do the work like regular kids, only to find that someone wanted to put him back in a special classroom. Frustrating—very frustrating."

He leaned back in his chair. "A few years ago there was a girl who had done just beautifully on the program. Sarah was her name. When her parents were ready to put her back into school, all of us on the staff prepared ourselves to write the hundreds of letters that it usually takes and to make a thousand phone calls. Several months passed and we didn't hear anything from Sarah's parents, so I called them to find out what happened.

" 'Nothing happened,' her mother told me. 'We just put her in school.'

" 'In a regular class?' I asked.

" 'In a regular class,' she answered.

" 'With her own age group?' I asked.

" 'With her own age group,' she answered.

" 'And the school gave you no problems?' I asked.

" 'No problems,' she answered.

"Well, I couldn't believe it. It was too good to be true. Then I grew very suspicious that Sarah's mother was not telling me everything, so I asked her how she got Sarah back in school without having problems.

"She paused for a moment, then answered, 'We cheated, Mr. Doman.'

"Now, Sarah's mother was a very quiet and polite woman—honest as the day is long. I couldn't believe my ears. 'What did you say?' I asked.

"Then she repeated her answer: 'We cheated.'

"'And how did you do that?" I wanted to know. She told me the most extraordinary story.

"She said, 'About the time we were ready to place Sarah in school, the company my husband works for transferred him to Seattle, Washington. After we moved and were settled in our new home, I took Sarah to the school and told them that she was supposed to be in the third grade. When they asked about her school records, I told them that they were on the way. They didn't question what I said, so they let Sarah begin school in the third grade. About a month later, the principal called and asked about the records again, and I told him I would check on them.'

"'Haven't they arrived yet?' I asked her.

"'Oh, Mr. Doman, there aren't any,' she answered. 'The school that Sarah went to in San Francisco burned down and the school records were burned with it. When I told the principal about that, he just said, 'That's too bad. We'll start some new ones.'

"That's all there was to it," Doman laughed.

"Sarah is in school and everything is just wonderful.

"I'll bet I told that story seven or eight times before I got the message," he said. "If your child's life is at stake, what's wrong with cheating?

"So we became schemers and plotters around here and we started getting kids in regular classes without big fights. Sometimes parents would say that their child had been required to stay home because of vision problems or hearing problems. We even outfitted some kids who didn't really need them with hearing aids. You see, the trick was to get them back in school without mentioning the brain." He stopped for a moment. "It's easier if there is no previous record on the child," he said, "but I see that Jeremiah was in a special education class for a while."

"Two months," Mother told him.

Mr. Doman sighed thoughtfully. "It may not be a problem, and then again it may. Some schools give our kids no trouble, but many still do. I think you might be wise to consider a move—not necessarily into another state but perhaps across town. Think about it."

"We will," Dad answered.

"Good," Mr. Doman said smiling. "If we get him fixed up, we don't want anybody looking at him and thinking he's brain-injured.

"Mr. and Mrs. Rodgers, there are brain-injured kids in almost all parts of this country and many parts of the world who are now in regular classes, and the teachers and the other students have no idea that these children were brain-injured."

I quickly thought of all the kids in my homeroom and wondered if maybe...just maybe ...no, it couldn't be...but then again...who knows, maybe one of those kids in my room was brain-injured and I never knew it.

"Now, then," Mr. Doman said, leaning forward, "if we intend to make this young man well, we don't have much time, do we? So we will have to work even harder than ever before."

"We will," my mother said.

Dad stood up, shook his head, and said, "I don't know what kind of magician you are, Mr. Doman. When we came in here, I was ready to tell you we were working too many hours and we had to have an easier program, and within a few minutes we're promising you that if you say so, we'll work even harder. And if you say so, I guess we'll pick up and move to only God knows where. Do most of the parents who come here do exactly as you people tell them?"

Mr. Doman smiled. "Most of them," he said. "There are some people who think that we're witches here and that we cast spells."

"I believe it," my father said, only half joking. "Are you a good witch or a bad one?"

"The answer to that depends on who you ask." Mr. Doman laughed.

"If Jeremiah gets well," I found myself saying, "then you must be good witches."

"I agree with that," Mr. Doman said, laughing.

We realized that another year lay ahead of us, a year that promised to be every bit as hard as the one we had just finished. But for the moment we forgot how tired we were. We were laughing and eager to begin again.

The picnic would have to wait another year.

Plateau Panic

When we returned home, we began the program with new energy. We were even more eager to see results because we thought the end was almost within our grasp.

The situation that developed in the next six months can best be described in two words— *plateau panic.*

As Jeremiah's abilities improved, we said that he had reached a new level of development. If for some reason he stayed at that level very long without noticeable improvement, we said he was on a plateau. Sometimes he might stay on a plateau for two or three weeks or maybe a month. At three weeks we started worrying. At five weeks we became frightened. When he plateaued for over five months there was out-and-out *panic.*

During the first month on the new program, Jeremiah progressed wonderfully. We thought, *Oh boy, at this rate he'll be well by Christmas— six months ahead of schedule.* Then things ground

215

to a halt. His walking didn't improve; his reading didn't progress; his hand coordination didn't get better. It was as if everything had stopped.

Mom called The Institutes several times to tell them about it. She was told that this sometimes happens, to keep working and he would probably come out of it. They said not to worry, but she did worry. We worried too.

Although we tried our best not to, we became greatly discouraged. That well little boy we had pictured for Jeremiah seemed farther and farther away from us. And finally, we almost lost sight of him.

"We might as well face it," Mother said one night after Jeremiah was asleep. "It's all over. He's gone as far as he can go."

"What do you mean?" Josh asked.

"She means that she doesn't think Jeremiah is going to get better," Dad replied.

"But Mr. Doman said a year," I reminded them.

"He meant a year of improvements," Mother said, "not a year of no changes."

"But he's been on plateaus before," I stressed.

"Never this long," Dad answered.

I was fresh out of arguments.

"Then what will we do?" I asked, not even wanting an answer.

"We'll do the program until his appointment at The Institutes," Mother said quietly.

All of us knew that that was only three weeks away.

"We Can't Go On"

"I understand that you've been having a difficult time," Mr. Doman said, coming straight to the point.

"We can't keep going on like this," Mother told him. "We can't see any improvements."

"I quite agree," Mr. Doman said.

"We've done the program every day just exactly as we were told to do it," Dad explained.

"I never for one minute questioned that," Mr. Doman replied. "I think you've done everything that you could possibly do."

"If we could see just a little more improvement," Mother said, "anything—then we would keep doing the program."

"I'm sure you would," Mr. Doman said sympathetically.

Then no one said anything for what seemed like ever so long a period of time.

Finally Mr. Doman spoke again. "Now that you won't be doing the program any longer, what are your plans?" he questioned.

"What?" Mother asked.

"Now that you won't be doing the program, what will you do?" he repeated.

"I don't know," she replied, thinking about it. "I don't know." She turned toward Dad. "What will we do?" she asked.

He didn't have an answer.

"Have you thought of the alternatives?" Mr. Doman asked. "For instance, you can place him in a special education classroom. . . ."

"I can't do that," Mother said, shaking her head.

"What are we going to do?" Dad said, thinking aloud.

Mother looked at Mr. Doman. "Has any other child ever been on a plateau for this long before?"

"Oh good heavens, yes," he answered.

"Have any stayed on a level any longer than six months?"

"Yes, indeed," he said, nodding his head.

"What did their parents do?" Dad asked.

"Some of them stopped."

"But some of them went on, is that right?" Mother asked.

"That's right," Mr. Doman answered. "Some of them went on."

"And among those parents who kept doing the program, did any of their kids improve later?" Dad asked.

"Yes."

"Did any of them not get well?" Dad wanted to know.

"Some of them did not," Mr. Doman replied.

"Mr. Doman," Mother said, leaning forward, "what do you think we should do?"

"I think you should do what you feel is best for Jeremiah," he answered. "I am a great believer in people making their own choices. If you want to stop the program right at this moment, I will fight for your right to do that. I will not, and no staff member here, will ever try to talk you into continuing if you want to stop."

"We're not saying that the program didn't help Jeremiah," Dad said, "because it did. Obviously he's much better now than he was a year ago."

"Obviously," Mr. Doman agreed.

"But as you yourself have said," Dad continued, "it's an extremely difficult program."

"Impossible," Mr. Doman said.

"No, it's not," Mother said suddenly. "It's not impossible, because we have done it. So it's not impossible."

"Well, *almost* impossible," Mr. Doman said.

"Look, I may have lost all of my senses, but what are we doing sitting here talking about how hard the program is or isn't? We all know it's rough," Mother said. "We've had it both ways with Jeremiah. We've lived without the program, and we've lived with the program. And rough as the program is, it's not nearly so bad as not having something to do...some plan...some goal. Look at us. We're all still here, and we're still strong. The program hasn't killed any of us and it hasn't worn us *all* the way down. It has just bent us a little. If the rest of you are willing, I'm willing to give it another try."

"I'll buy that," Dad said.

"And what about you two?" Mr. Doman said, looking at Josh and me.

"I never wanted to quit in the first place," Josh replied.

"I don't want to stop either," I answered.

"And what about you, young man?" Mr. Doman asked, looking at Jeremiah. "What do you want?"

Without the slightest hesitation, Jeremiah answered, "I want to drive a car."

"I'm with you, kid," Mr. Doman said. Then he laughed. "Well, Mr. and Mrs. Rodgers, it's been a long war. We've won a few battles and we've lost a few. The setbacks always hurt more than the victories. It's a lot more fun to win. So I guess we'd better try to win. While you are here this week, the staff will go over your program with a fine-tooth comb. By the end of the week, we may have changed the program a great deal or maybe not at all. But whatever we do it will be our very best."

"Thank you," Mother said, reaching out her hand.

"Not at all, Mrs. Rodgers," he replied. "It is my privilege. I am completely convinced that I'm the luckiest man alive. It is my extreme pleasure to see parents such as you and to work with kids like Jeremiah. It's my privilege, indeed."

As we left his office, I glanced back at Mr. Doman standing in the doorway. I thought for a moment there were tears in his eyes. I liked him.

Fast Motion

If fate had a great sense of drama, I envisioned that on Christmas morning we would awaken to find Jeremiah completely well. But that was not to be the case.

We did all the patternings ourselves on Christmas Day. Jeremiah was excited over his new toys, especially the police car that one of the patterners had left for him. The rest of us were in a dumpy mood, and we seemed to keep getting more restless as the evening wore on.

Finally Mother said, "I think I'm going to lose my mind if Jeremiah doesn't turn off that siren."

Suddenly all of us realized what she had said. We turned and looked at each other. He wasn't afraid of the siren. For the first time in his life, Jeremiah was enjoying a loud noise.

"I don't know if that's a good change or not," Mother said, contemplating future days filled with siren noises.

The rest of us knew exactly how she felt.

It seemed that from that time on everything began to happen in fast motion—like a movie when the projector is speeded up.

Jeremiah could button his shirt.

He could run without falling down.

He could throw a ball.

And wonder of wonders, he could catch it too.

He started reading all the signs along the streets.

He read a book (a little one, but it was a book).

He could write his own name.

He could write the names of all of us in the family.

He could write his own address and telephone number.

The lights were turning on, not by ones and twos; they must have been turning on by the tens and the hundreds!

That spring was the greatest ever! I can't remember ever seeing Mom and Dad in happier moods. Sometimes Mother just stood and watched as Jeremiah played with the other children in the neighborhood. He seemed to learn their games in no time, and soon his coordination was so good that no one could have singled him out from the other children. He looked like them; he acted like them; he *was* like them.

Jeremiah Rodgers was going to win!

New Plans

As summer neared, Mother thought that it was time to plan ahead toward Jeremiah's future. She called and made an appointment with Mr. McNulty, the grade school principal.

When she met with him, she told him what wonderful improvements Jeremiah had made and said that she would like to enroll him in school the following year.

Then she asked him what she really wanted to know.

"Is it possible to withhold from his teacher the information that Jeremiah was brain-injured and that he was once in a special education class?" she asked.

"That's doubtful," Mr. McNulty replied.

"I don't mean to falsify the records," Mother stressed. "I mean, just not have that information *in* the record, so that Jeremiah can have a clean start like all the other children."

"I know what you mean," Mr. McNulty replied, "but the records have very little to do with it. Mrs. Rodgers, your family is quite well known in the community. There has been a lot of talk about Jeremiah's program. Since both M.J. and Josh have gone to school here, there has been talk at the school too. If we leave that off his record, his teacher is bound to find out some other way."

"I hadn't thought of that," Mother said. "Of course, you are right."

That night Mother and Dad talked it over and they decided that we would move.

Josh wasn't happy about this and neither was I. We would have to leave our friends and move somewhere where we would be strangers and not know anyone. In some ways the thought of moving seemed more difficult than beginning the program had seemed.

Besides, the decision had *not* been reached by democratic action. There had been *no* family meeting called to discuss it. It was an out-and-out act of dictators.

Mother was just as demanding when she went to Dr. Zefrelli's office.

"Will you please write a letter," she asked, "stating that Jeremiah is a year late in beginning school because he had a vision problem?"

"But Mrs. Rodgers, there were other problems, too," the doctor replied.

"I'm quite aware of what they were," Mother said matter-of-factly. "He had hearing problems, feeling problems, walking problems, talking problems—in fact, what Jeremiah had was a brain problem. But if you put that in your letter, there is a good chance that the people who read it will look at him differently than they will if they're told only that he had an eye problem."

"Some people wouldn't," he argued.

"That may be true," Mother replied. "But we don't know, do we? I don't wish to stake Jeremiah's future on the possibility that only the right people will read your letter. Do you?"

He didn't answer.

"It's not as if I'm asking you to lie," she said. "The truth is, he did have a vision problem. I simply don't want you to clutter the letter with all those other things."

Dr. Zefrelli wrote the letter.

After weeks of interviews and letters, Dad found a job that didn't pay quite as much as the one he had, but as Dad said, "They can't keep a bright guy down. By the end of the year, I'll be president of the company."

In July we moved.

Good-bye, Alice...

And Karen...

And Margery....

Good-bye, house on Maple Street.

Good-bye, Indianapolis.

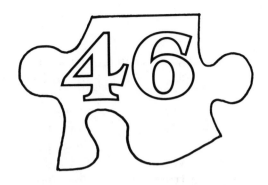

The Last Chapter

I'm sure that a great writer would have described our move in vivid detail--the last look at our house, the last words to a dear friend, each moment a gem captured in words--but I've never proposed that I was a great writer. Besides, I don't want to think of those things. Not now. Maybe someday in the distant future after all the wounds have healed and the tears have dried, I may once again take up the pen and write about those traumas.

And I suppose a better writer would describe with great emotional impact Jeremiah's first day at school. That really wouldn't be very difficult to do, because it was a day of a thousand emotions. It was a great victory. And it was a proud moment.

227

at this moment it is tempting to write that this extraordinary moment in Jeremiah's life was the result of a lot of work by many people -- Glenn Doman and the staff members at The Institutes, and over fifty people who patterned my brother. It is also tempting to mention that it is the result of two years of minutes, ~~hours~~, and hours and days and months taken from our lives... and ~~postponed picnics~~. And it would be right to say that the one person who gave more hours and more days than anyone else was Mother. Those would be easy things to say because they are all true.

I would rather tell of a day about a month after Jeremiah started to school. I love this scene because it tells so much.

When Mother went for the first meeting with Jeremiah's teacher, she was more than a little nervous. She had been to many parent-teacher conferences before to talk with Josh's and my teachers. However, this time was a bit different.

"Mrs. Rodgers, so nice to meet you," Mrs. Adams said. "Please come in."

Mother followed Mrs. Adams to the chairs which were waiting by a short, round table.

"I want to tell you how much I enjoy having Jeremiah in my class," Mrs. Adams said.

"Thank you," Mother replied.

"I noticed on Jeremiah's records that he is one

228

year late in starting first grade."

"Yes," Mother answered, trying not to show her concern.

"Because of a vision problem, it says. . . ."

"Yes."

"Mrs. Rodgers," the teacher said with direct-ness, "is there anything special about his visual problems that might be helpful to him if I knew?"

"What do you mean?" Mother asked.

"I mean would it be better if I had him sit closer to the chalkboard or should I take any special notice of him when he is on the playground?"

"No," Mother answered quietly, "nothing special."

"Good," Mrs. Adams said. "It's a shame that he had to wait a year to start school. Jeremiah's such a bright child."

At last Mother relaxed and smiled. "Yes, he is," she said.

Some people may think that we gave up too much—too much time and too much energy for my brother. I suppose that would depend upon how much they think the life of one little boy is worth. To us, Jeremiah was worth two years.

Some people might think that Josh and I might have felt terribly insecure because our parents paid so much attention to our brother's problems. I think it was just the opposite. It made us feel more secure. If they did it for Jeremiah, then surely they would do the same for one of us.

Some people may think that Jeremiah might never fully appreciate what we did. I don't know about how Josh feels, but personally I think a little appreciation goes a long way. If someone thanked me every day for the rest of my life, it would make me sick at my stomach.

One time we were reminiscing about how the patterners used to come every day and what lovely people they were. Jeremiah looked up and said, "I dreamed about that once, *a long time ago.*" How much more of a thank-you would anyone want?

a Final Note —

You may be wondering why I haven't mentioned where we moved. I can't. My lips and my pen have been sealed by an act of dictators.

It was agreed that I would be allowed to write this book if I didn't tell things which might affect our futures, such as where we live or our real names. Well, now that's out of the bag! Our real name isn't Rodgers. (Sorry about that.) Josh's name isn't really Josh; Jeremiah's name, of course, has been changed to protect the innocent and the guilty.

And my name — oh, well, what's the difference? What's in a name? By name now, you know more about my family than names and places could ever tell. You know about our hopes and our fears, our joys and our sorrows. You know about our ideas and our goals.

Most important, you know that somewhere

in this country, perhaps even in the city where you live, there is a ~~boy~~ little boy attending school, and no one in his classroom suspects that he was once a boy called _hopeless_.

A Final, Final Note—

I have to hurry—Dad's raising a storm out in the car, honking his horn. Don't you just love happy endings? I do. And ours is happy -- well, almost. Thanks to "Josh's" influence, it looks like "Jeremiah" is going to be a shortstop. That's all we needed in our house—another baseball freak. Zap! Well, ~~we~~ you can't win 'em all.

Everyone else is in the car. If I don't rush, they'll leave without me. The basket is packed. I made the potato salad; Mother fried the chicken. Grandmother is visiting with us, so she baked the pies. As you probably guessed, we're going on a picnic.

There goes the horn again. Sounds like Dad means it ~~this~~ time. Gotta go!

Take care,

M. J.

Ralph Miller is Back to Back

and the fun is about to begin!

"RALPH MILLER is a children's book and for adults too. It is cleverly written, simple and hilarious — completely satisfying — a small masterpiece!"
— **Philip A. Sadler**
Professor of Children's Literature, CMSU

"The sequel of RALPH MILLER extends satire into farce and makes readers laugh and think at the same time. It's an absolute delight!"
— **Kaye Anderson, Ph.D.**
Editor, The IRA MISSOURI READER

Now published by

LANDMARK EDITIONS

1420 Kansas Avenue
Kansas City, Missouri 64127